I0708881

MASKED

All Rights Reserved
Copyright Fanny Garstang
First Edition 2023
Cover Art by Steven Johnson

Everyone deserves a bit of happiness. I hope you find yours
as Viktor finds his.

PROLOGUE

The bear's claw had raked diagonally across the ten year old's face. He was brought in screaming and howling in pain. Blood and the clear vitreous fluid of his left eye ran down his face from where the bear's claw had ripped open the eye. The other was badly scratched.

While his mother went to her son, Count Tverdislav Nikolavich Medvedev loaded a pistol himself. He walked out to the now calm juvenile brown bear. It didn't matter that the bear had probably been roused up by his son. It had injured him and it wouldn't be allowed to do it again. He pulled back the pistol's hammer and at point blank range shot the bear in the head. He turned away and handed the pistol to the shocked bear keeper, "bury it. I don't want to see it. You can collect your wages tomorrow as we won't be having another bear."

He walked back into the family's large house on the family estate and to the nursery rooms where his son gulped and whimpered. He stood in the doorway, "never again Daria. No more bears. I don't care if it's the tradition of the family."

"What have we done to anger God?" She looked at her husband with fear etched on her face.
He crossed the room to her and put a hand on his wife's shoulder. They watched as their daughters' nursemaid cleaned his face.

They all turned as an old woman dressed in the plain clothes of a serf was brought in. She was wearing a clean apron over a coarse woven blouse and sarafan, a blue pinafore dress with embroidered straps. She was shown in looking nervous. The Count's manservant said, "she's the local medicine woman sir."

"Sir." She curtseyed, bending on aching knees, to her lord.

"He has to live." The Countess ordered.

"I can't promise anything." She said cautiously, glancing nervously around.

"Then do what you can." The Count retorted.
She approached the bed, "I need clean gut, a sharp needle and a flame."
The countess nodded, "of course." She gestured for the nursery maid to go find what was requested, "get the needle from my sewing box." She turned to her husband and added, ignoring the serf's presence, "we must get a doctor from St Petersburg." She looked intently at her husband's servant who was lingering behind her husband. The servant looked to his master who gave him the nod to obey.

The household waited fearfully for the death or survival of the direct family's heir. The girls and their younger son were kept away in their school room and shared bedroom while his parents drifted in and out of their eldest's room watching as he fought the fever. Daria turned as her husband entered the room. She gripped the end of the bed while the priest prayed over her silvery ash blonde haired son. Responding to the end of the prayer they both murmured, "amen."
Tverdislav put an arm round his wife as she said, "if he survives he will be ridiculed. No one will want to marry him. We mustn't allow this to get out. We will have to create a way of hiding the disfigurement."

"Let us remain optimistic. St Paraskevi will be watching over him."

"He had such beautiful grey eyes. It isn't fair Tverdislav. He's only a little boy."

"We will try and keep his life as normal as we can. It will be hard but we have to try."

"We could try for another." She suggested, looking up
with red rimmed eyes, preparing herself for him to die.
Although she had been a good wife and carried ten children
only four lived, two girls and two boys. The last two
pregnancies had ended in miscarriages.

CHAPTER 1

1757

He survived. He grew up with his sisters but was never seen by anyone other than his direct family. He was kept confined to a suite of rooms within the family's house in St Petersburg.

His education came to an abrupt end. The angry boy turned into an angry young man as he continued to struggle with the loss of his sight into adulthood. The only man who managed to engage the young man was his fencing master.

It had taken a year for him to get back to the skill level had had been before he lost his sight and was now as good as his father who he practiced with. Now he could sense when the attack was happening through the movement of the air and the sounds of his opponent. He had enough sight in his right eye that when he wasn't wearing a mask he could see the silhouette of whoever was in front of him.

When not practising his sword skills with either a rapier or a shashka, a Russian single edged sabre with no handguard he was listening to his sisters reading to him in his two roomed suite. He wasn't left completely alone as he had a manservant and a large Samoyed, a black and white furred dog with a tail that curled on to its back.

His sisters, especially Tamara, were determined to improve him by reading everything they could lay their hands on. It didn't always work as the masks, that hid his disfigured face, allowed him to fall asleep. Only Tamara was not fooled but she wasn't around much now as she had her own family.

For the moment his dog lay at Viktor's feet as Alla,

his youngest sister and youngest of the now three surviving siblings, read to him. She sat casually with her stocking feet tucked under the skirt of her dark red long sleeved dress where she sat cross legged on the settle opposite her brother. She brushed strands of brown hair out of her eyes as she concentrated on the page of printed words, squinting.

Viktor knew it was her as she had a monotonous voice as if reading to him was a chore. Behind one of many velvet and silk masks made by his mother his eyelids closed over an eye that could only discern between light and dark; and a glass eye in his empty eye socket.

He woke up when he heard the door open and Tamara's footsteps. He heard her say with a teasing tone, "Alla, you'd best stop reading. You can send anyone to sleep with your voice and I'm sure Viktor was almost asleep just now."

"It is so tedious reading to him." Alla replied as if her brother wasn't in the room.

Alla blamed her brother that she still hadn't married and was going to become a spinster like their great aunt who was just as tedious to be around as she also had to be read to as she couldn't read. The sisters were lucky that their father had decided they should all learn to read and write, empowered by the fact Peter the Great had educated his own daughters though it was rumoured that Empress Elizabeth Petrova could neither read nor write herself as she had refused to learn as a child. Peter the Great had introduced Russia to the ways of Western Europe and they wouldn't be turning their backs any time soon.

"Don't say such things especially when Viktor is in the room. I think you'd best go." Tamara said sternly. Viktor heard a sigh of relief from Alla and then her footsteps leave the room.

Tamara, dressed in a simple plain black skirt of fine wool and a long sleeved blouse with white flowers embroidered on it; crossed the room to her little brother. She placed a sisterly kiss on his cheek and straightened his mask.

She smiled at him with his pale blonde hair and clean shaven narrow chiselled face. He looked like a younger version of their father. His current plain brown coat and waistcoat hid the muscular body of a swordsman. Although plain they were still of good quality. He never went anywhere so didn't need anything fancier.

He pulled his mask up and rubbed his face. The scars used to be red and angry but over the years had faded to skin colour but they were still raised and obvious from the stitching of muscles and skin all that time ago. When they were dry and tight they itched. He knew Tamara wouldn't be offended.

Tamara claimed Alla's seat and tutted at the abandoned slip on shoes before she said, "don't worry about her. I have more interesting things to tell you than a musty book in German."
He asked stiffly, "what is that then?"
"Mother is organising a party for your birthday and she's going to invite all the eligible women to finally find you a wife."
Viktor was quiet. He knew that a planned betrothal had been cancelled back when he was ten at the same time as his younger brother became the heir to the family name until he foolishly died by falling through thin ice on the Neva the previous winter. Now his mother would have to find him a wife, the right wife, which would be hard for her.

He knew his father worried for his future and the family's now that he had become heir again. They weren't particularly wealthy after spending a bit too much money in response to Peter the Great's demand that the nobility move to St Petersburg as it was being built. Their grandfather had invested in building supplies and sold them on but hadn't been paid for all of it. The only compensation they got was a plot of land to build a Dacha, ideal for getting away from the stinking city in the summer since it was built on a swamp near the mouth of the Neva as it flowed into the Baltic, when they weren't on the family estate North of the city.

Tamara may have said it was a party for him but he knew he wouldn't be attending. He heard the settle creak as Tamara leant forward. She asked with concern, "aren't you excited?"

"You say it's a party for me but I won't be there. I'm too much of an embarrassment for mother. I'm just a burden to everyone." He replied bitterly.

"Just Alla thinks that." She tried to reassure him while recognising a change in his mood, wanting to stop it before the anger got any worse, "I care for you and I don't think you are a burden."

"But you aren't here all the time. You have your own family to look after. I know our servants would just ignore me and let me starve if they could."

"Oh Viktor, don't do this. Mother and father dote on you."

"Don't do what? Don't do this?" He shouted. He found the corner of the side table that had previously been repaired. He stood and turned it over, sending a jug of watered-down red wine and a glass across the floor. The dog jumped up and barked in alarm. Viktor went on, "strange way of showing it then, keeping me hidden away. I don't want to be treated like an invalid who can't dress myself and need someone to cut up my food for me." He staggered and found the back of a chair and threw it in the direction of Tamara which fell short, crashing to the floor and breaking a leg on it.

She tried to calm him though she choked on a sob, "they just don't want you to get hurt by others' words." She hated it when he had his mood swings, swinging wily from depression to rage and in recent years what made it worse was their mother's reaction. She continued to treat him like a child… And here she came. Tamara was frustrated for her brother.

Countess Daria Ivanova Medvedeva swept into the room wearing clothes similarly to her daughter's but with a shawl wrapped round herself. Her greying hair was up in a simple bun as she hadn't been out visiting. She caught the end of her son's outburst, "I'm ugly and a freak. I will be the end of the direct line and everyone will whisper amongst themselves saying it was the disfigurement that kept every woman at bay. Valentin shouldn't have gone skating so late in the season."
The Countess glared at Tamara as she took Viktor in her arms though he fought her, his anger at its height. He protested, "go away, don't touch me."

"Ssh Viktor." Daria said softly as she brushed his hair off his flustered face. He moaned and leant against her as they both sank to the floor. Viktor could feel his mother's amber necklace pressing against his face and could smell her sweet perfume. Tears ran down his face as he gasped for breath and moaned, "it hurts."
Daria looked to her daughter, "get the doctor sent for."

Tamara released her held breath and willingly fled the room. She hated it when Viktor had what his mother politely called 'one of his fits.' They feared them. They came out as a rage where even the Count had been hurt trying to control his son.

When the doctor arrived he found Viktor curled up on the carpet with the Countess knelt beside her son. She looked relieved to see him. The doctor remarked, "his brain

has become inflamed again?"
The Countess nodded.

  "Then I'll give him a sleeping draught so he rests and I'll draw some blood to bring the inflammation down."

Viktor's eyes widened. He didn't want to rest and he didn't want the bloodletting to happen. He sat upright and exclaimed, "no!"
He staggered to his feet and his servant grabbed him. Koplev, a man from the estate who was strong enough to hold Viktor down, was of serf stock with a large black moustache he was proud of. Viktor weakly fought the servant's strong grip as he was led to his bedroom.

He didn't want to be treated like an invalid. He wanted to wallow in the self-pity that followed his rage. The dog barked as it sensed his growing anger at his mother and the doctor. He twisted his head back and forth as he heard the sleeping draught being stirred, a spoon clinking on glass. Daria said sternly, "behave Viktor. He's here to help you. Koplev, hold him still."
Viktor gave up the fight as Koplev held down his arms and Daria held his head still. Reluctantly he drank the draught and heard breaths being released as he submitted himself to sleep. The bloodletting was quickly done and then the doctor was shown out.

The Countess sat on the edge of the dishevelled bed, the sheets twisted from where Viktor had struggled. A bloodstain on the linen and the torn sleeve was the evidence of the bloodletting. She removed his coat that currently hung over one shoulder and his buckled shoes. She pulled a blanket over his stockinged legs. As she did she glanced up at the large gold haloed icon of St Paraskvei holding a bowl with a pair of eyes in it and a cross. She sent up a silent prayer to the saint to watch over her little boy.

No matter how hard she tried she couldn't see the man he had become. She wanted to keep him locked away

from a world that would mock him and turn its back on
him. She wanted to keep him safe from harm and from
those who would take advantage of him but she also knew
that Viktor was now heir and he would have to be allowed
to step up into that role. She brushed hair from his damp
scarred forehead and kissed it, "I do this for you, always for
you. I never want to see you suffering or hurt by anyone."

CHAPTER 2

The evening of Viktor's birthday party arrived. He sat on a chair in a window alcove behind a curtain dressed in a red and gold coat and waistcoat with his dog, Borya, at his feet. He heard the voices of the guests over the musicians. He was attending his party but no one apart from his family knew he was hidden behind the ceiling to floor curtains, his back against the closed shutters. Most of the guests were there to be seen and enjoy the rare hospitality of the Medvedev family. Curiosity had brought some of them to the party as they knew of the son's death and they wondered who they were going to present as the new heir to the name.

The throats and hair of the women were glittering with jewels as they fluttered round talking to friends, their silk and satin skirts rustling over the marble floors. A few men wore military uniform but otherwise most wore embroidered knee length frock coats and waistcoats with silk stockings and knee length breeches. All the fashion was influenced by the French as decreed by Peter the Great and his daughter Elizabeth. The rooms were bright with the hundreds of candelabras that showed off the marble, gold painted plaster and framed paintings of the townhouse, showing off the wealth, some of it discreetly rented.

The rooms went quiet as the guests were led to dinner. Koplev slipped behind the curtain and announced himself, "time to go upstairs sir."
Viktor stood and held out a hand. Koplev placed his master's hand on his shoulder and led him upstairs and back to his suite of rooms where he would be served his own dinner.

*

Nastasia Balakina glanced at herself in a tall mirror and tucked a wisp of hair behind her ear. She adjusted her necklace of gold and amber and smiled. She smoothed out an imagery crease in the outer skirt of her pale green floral printed silk square necked dress as she sat down next to her friend and half sister. The skirt was open at the front to reveal the plain underskirt in the same colour. She watched the dancing men and women over the top of her fan through warm golden brown eyes. She asked, "anyone take your fancy Katerina?"

"Don't be silly Nastasia." Katerina said from behind her own fan.

They looked very similar with their dark brown hair piled high on their heads and slim pale necks. What marked them out as being different was Katerina wore a ribbon choker with a large cut emerald on it which matched her green eyes and her hair had a string of pearls woven through it. Her square necked dress was of the finest green silk brocade covered in gold flowers.

"Oh come, you can't remain your father's keeper forever." Katerina smiled softly at her half sister. Nastasia was half recognised by the father they shared but only enough to be companion to his legitimate daughter. Nastasia was his daughter by his long time mistress. He gave her money for an education of sorts and clothes but she wasn't allowed to use his name.

Nastasia went on, "wouldn't you like to marry? Isn't that what we are here for? You have it easy while I have to fight to earn my respectability. They know who my mother is and all I'll achieve is some younger son if at all or will have to lower myself even further to some lowly officer."

They were interrupted by a thirty-year-old in uniform, "miss Nastasia, will you dance?"

15

Nastasia turned her scathing golden-brown eyes on to the intruder though it didn't stop her from aching her back a little to make her bosom more prominent. Oh, she did like to tease the men, "haven't I already told you Igor Petrovich that I don't wish to dance? I'm having a rest from dancing, maybe later." She lowered her fan and gave him a bewitching smile.

He bowed and mumbled, "later then."

"You tease." Katerina exclaimed in mock horror.

"He's terrible at dancing. Now, where were we? Since we are at the Medvedevs' do you know if they have another son? Didn't they lose their heir last year? I haven't seen nor heard of there being another. They aren't normally ones to hold a party in their home. Wasn't the last one for their youngest coming of age not that she has married yet." Nastasia asked conspiratorially.

Katerina leant closer, "there is one but he is rarely seen."

"How come?"

"That's all I know. I overheard my father discussing the family with one of my brothers. I think there had once been plans for me to marry him."

"They are thinking of marriage again if they are holding this party." Nastasia remarked, observing all the young single girls present, "so he has to be here somewhere. Maybe he has been away on a tour of Europe like our noble Tsar did, and now he's back. Do you know what he looks like?"

"I've never seen a portrait or heard a description of him."

"He wasn't at dinner as I recognised most of the faces. Let's go see if we can find him." Nastasia stood determined to get her meeker half-sister involved in something other than running her father's household for him. She was surprised she hadn't been snapped up already as the fact she ran it so well made her prime marriage material… but maybe also that was why their father hadn't let go of her already.

There must have been some dealings between the two families recently that had potentially brought the idea back to the fore. She knew that the Medvedevs were traders as well as lower aristocracy only having held their titles a few generations due to some deed they did for the Romanovs in the past. They used the resources on their large estate near Moscow to supply both Moscow and St Petersburg with the building supplies the cities needed.

"I should let my father know where I am."

"Don't be silly. He's probably in the salon with the other fathers leaving the mothers to chaperone us girls, or in our case each other." Nastasia pulled Katerina up, "I don't think he's down here as there is no talk of him so let's go upstairs."

"Maybe he's in with the men? He's got to be in his late twenties, right?"

"The mothers would all be talking if he was down here, you know that. Come on, some of them are eyeing you up for their sons." Nastasia pointed out.

Pulled along by her bold half sister Katerina found herself unable to say no. They left the brightly lit ballroom and no one stopped them from heading upstairs as others were drifting into the cooler withdrawing room for more talk or a game of cards

At the top of the stairs they entered a suite of rooms, where the door was ajar, which was designed towards a man tastes with paintings of hunting on the dark green walls and with a rack of several rapiers, shashkas and an orient saber. The next room was painted a pale yellow to make it as light as possible. At a small table in the window was a man with pale silver-blonde hair eating his dinner, reaching for the glass of wine. At his feet a dog growled. The man reached down and tugged at the curled tail as he called out, "who's there?"

The young women were taken by surprise that it was a young man who spoke.

"Oh, please excuse us." Katerina said, "we'll leave."

"No, don't." He turned in his chair, "come and sit. I don't get many visitors."

"We should go back downstairs." Katerina whispered behind her fan.

Nastasia whispered, "this could be him. Come on." She headed across the room.

With a roll of her eyes and a sigh Katerina followed.

At the table Viktor gestured, "there should be a settle opposite so don't hesitate to sit. Who are you? I don't recognise the footsteps."

They realised then that he wore a mask across his face. They glanced at each other, was this the reason no one knew much about the new Medvedev heir? Nastasia was disappointed, he was deformed, but she was still curious. She asked, "who are you?"

"Viktor Tvedislavich Medvedev. And yourselves?"

"Katerina Livovna Kolesova and Nastasia Balakina." Katerina answered.

"Who is your father Nastasia?"

"I cannot say sir if you are not aware of who I am." Nastasia said reluctantly and then more brightly to get away from the touchy subject she added, "I do believe the party downstairs is for your birthday."

"It is." Viktor answered stiffly, "are you enjoying it?"

"Yes." Katerina said with a glance at her sister who was frowning, "may I ask why you are not down there?"

"I have been ill recently." Viktor lied.

Nastasia looked suspiciously at him, knowing he was lying, but didn't say anything.

The three of them fell into an uncomfortable silence while below the musicians played. The young women wondered what was hidden behind the cloth mask while

Viktor didn't know how to even start a conversation. He wondered what the two women were even doing in his room. He cleared his throat and opened his mouth to say something but then closed it again. Katerina shifted in the silence and softly said, "we should perhaps go back downstairs."

Though they had barely said any words between them Viktor sadly said, "perhaps you should. I am not great company."

He listened to the retreating footsteps and felt alone again. He had sensed their curiosity and disgust and wished they could see that his blindness didn't define him. His servant entered the room and asked, "who were they?"

"Party guests…." He and his servant had an odd relationship. Koplev was the closest thing to a confidante he had but the fact he was a servant hung over them a lot of the time. He added, "I couldn't think of anyway for them to stay."

"You could have offered them a drink sir?"

Viktor didn't reply as he pushed food round his plate with his fork.

Nastasia and Katerina returned downstairs. Nastasia remarked with a hint of disgust, "he's obviously disfigured somehow and how shy was he?"

"Give him a chance. We surprised him." Katerina answered in defence.

"Why should I? You are welcome to him."

"How can you judge him before you know him?" Katerina accused her sister.

"You know that rumours are enough to damage a woman's reputation. If my name became associated with his then no one else will want me." Nastasia declared, "come on, let's go find some healthy young men and have a dance."

Katerina stared in shock. She knew how self-centred her sister could be but still it always took her by surprise. But she understood why as Nastasia was a bastard and needed to appear respectable if she was to make a good marriage in a world where she was disapproved of by many.

Though she danced with a young man Nastasia's mind wasn't with him as her partner tried to make small talk. She had told her sister she wasn't interested but she was in fact intrigued. She wanted to know why he was hidden away and what his disfigurement was. And maybe, just maybe, his family would be desperate enough that they would marry her to him and then she really would be respectable and no one would be able to challenge her over her illegitimacy.

CHAPTER 3

Tamara decided she needed to get her brother away from the family home and their overprotective mother. Now he was the heir he needed to get out and be seen. Their mother couldn't keep him a recluse any longer. She suggested the idea to her husband who objected, "I don't want our children frightened by him. What about his fits?" It was better to use his children as an excuse then admit he didn't like his brother-in-law. He thought he behaved like an immature boy in a man's body. He thought his own children behaved more maturely than Viktor. The man needed to grow a backbone. He was a talented swordsman even if he was blind and should be using the skill to get out of the house and make something of himself. At least Empress Anna hadn't learnt of him or he would have been added to her collection of freaks.

"They won't be. They have seen him many times and he has his masks to hide the scars and I'll make sure no fits happen. I want to get him away from our mother. She is too protective of him."
Her husband looked grumpy, his mouth all squeezed up in his reluctance, "he's your brother, nothing to do with me. As long as he doesn't cause any trouble. You do as you please anyway." He sighed at the end.

"Thank you Gravil." She said with relief. She gave him a tight smile, "I'll go tell him." She gave him a kiss on the cheek but he twisted his head round and it became one on her lips.

She withdrew and he frowned in disappointment. He adored his strong-willed wife but knew she didn't feel the same. She submitted to his attentions as a dutiful wife should and had birthed his children and she had an affection for him but that was it. He looked after her wistfully as she headed to the family home. He tried to be a man and not be jealous of his wife's brother. She gave him more love and attention than he ever got and wanted it for himself. Sometimes he contemplated banning his wife from visiting but knew that would make the tension in his home even worst. Instead he debated just hanging out at the barracks more.

Tverdislav approved of the idea of Viktor going to his sister's. Daria was not so sure. She wanted to keep her son safe but for once her husband overruled her. He saw the sense in Tamara's reasoning and maybe Viktor's mood would improve if he spent some time with his niece and nephews before the subject of a wife was brought up. He was unaware that his daughter had already revealed the new family objective.

Viktor let Tamara help him into her carriage and tuck furs around him against the Russian biting winter. As the horses started off down the road Tamara revealed a surprise, "there is a ball coming up at court."
Viktor gave Borya's head a rub as he said with disinterest, "that's nice." It wasn't like he would be going.
   "It's a masked ball." She preserved.
   "Don't bother telling me any more Tamara as you know I won't be going." He remarked sorely.
   "Listen, I'm telling you for a reason. You are staying with us so that means you can come with us to the ball and mother can't stop you." She said conspiratorially.
He brightened at the thought of going to a ball but then fear took over, "how will they react around me. There will be so many people there and they will probably stare at me and I won't know any of them. I can't eat without making a mess and what about the end? Doesn't everyone reveal themselves?"
   "I'll be there." She tried to reassure him.

He went on as if he hadn't heard her, "they'll quickly realise I can't see."

"Viktor! Stop." She found one of his hands under the furs and gave it a squeeze. In a calmer voice, "I'll be there to look after you." She went on brightly to pull him away from the threatening 'fit' of frustration, "we are nearly there and your nephews and niece will be waiting to greet you."

Though he couldn't see them, two boys and a girl stood at the top of the stairs by the open front door with their nursemaid behind them. The twin boys ran across and grabbed a hand each and led their uncle into their home and into their mother's sitting room. Their ten year old sister walked beside her mother, thinking of herself as a grown up. The twins sat Viktor down before asking in unison, "have you brought us anything?"

"Lev, Ilya what have I told you before about demanding presents?" Tamara said with warning to her two six year old sons.

Viktor smiled, "it's alright Tamara. There should be some marzipan in one of my bags. Go ask Koplev to get it out for you."

He heard his nephews run off and with their footsteps a fading sound Viktor turned in the direction he had last heard his sister, "thank you for letting me come."

"I knew you needed to get away from mother. I know Alla isn't the best company and at least the twins don't care you can't see."

"Like their mother." He smiled, "Anna does as well. Where are you Anna? Aren't you going to greet your uncle?" He held out a hand.

She walked to him and curtseyed as she shyly said, "uncle." She put a hand cautiously in his and he gave it a squeeze.

"There's a little something for you as well in my bags."

He smiled, "why don't you go find out"

"Go on Anna." Tamara said, pushing her daughter towards the door. With her daughter gone she remarked, "don't say such things Viktor, you are embarrassing me."

"It is true though. You make me feel as if I am a man and not a child to be hidden away. I hope I might get a wife like you one day."

"Maybe you'll meet someone at the masked ball if our parents haven't decided on a wife for you yet." She commented as she handed him a black tea in a glass within a silver holder, into his two hands. He lifted it to his lips and took a sip from it.

The twins returned and they said in unison, "thank you uncle Viktor."

"What are they?" He asked.

"Mice." Tamara answered with a smile as she saw Lev bite the head off his. Ilya was having to push Borya away as it was having a sniff at the boy's mouse. She added, "you shouldn't have. They'll get all sticky and won't want their dinner."

"Oh leave them be. They'll have to grow up soon enough but let them have fun while they can." Viktor remarked good humouredly, "can I have a taste one of you?" He opened his mouth and Ilya put a piece of his mouse in his uncle's mouth. They giggled as he said, "meow, yum yum. Nothing quite like a mouse for a cat like me."

Tamara smiled as she watched her sons pop another piece of marzipan into their uncle's mouth who commented, "meow. I'll grow fat and won't be able to hunt again." Tamara couldn't help laughing then. She was glad she had brought Viktor to her home. Already there was colour in his usually pale cheeks as he enjoyed the happy company of his nephews. She was also proud of how her sons were interacting with their uncle. They didn't care he was blind. She worried about her daughter who sat opposite nibbling

at her mouse and glancing nervously at her uncle. She
looked embarrassed to be in the same room as Viktor and
Tamara wondered what she had heard or seen to make her
so.

Although he had been excited at the thought of
attending a masked ball of the almost completed Winter
Palace on the afternoon of the event Viktor was nervous.
Sitting in the carriage with Tamara and her husband he
asked with worry, "what should I do if I have to ask
someone to dance? If people ask who I am what do I say?
What about dinner?"
"Don't worry about it Viktor, just enjoy yourself." She
tried to reassure him. She ignored Gravil's rolling eyes and
tut of exasperation.
"How though?"
"I will worry about everything else."
"I can't let you do that." He objected.
"That is what you have had to let us do for most of your
life." She pointed out, "I'll always be nearby." She leant
across and gave his gloved hand a squeeze, showing she
had confidence in him, "just enjoy yourself."
"I'll try."
"Much of it is spent talking anyway or sitting listening to
some performers or watching a piece of theatre." Gravil
dressed in the dark green uniform of a Preobrazhensky
officer with red facings, collar and cuffs edged with white
piping, entered the conversation with a voice that relayed
how not thrilled he was to be going to another ball at the
palace. He could only hope to find a group of his fellow
officers who would be more interested in a smoke and a
game of cards. He'd leave Tamara to play nursemaid with
her brother.
As a small group they moved through the rooms
until they come to the large ball room. Crystal chandeliers

covered in candles glittered while mirrors reflected the light of more that were on multi branched candelabras that stood on the floor Rooms glittered with gold leaf and highly polished marble in the reflected candlelight.. Some rooms still smelt of wet paint and uncured plaster. Doors opened on to unfinished rooms where a few workman had fallen asleep and others had stored building equipment. This was a palace designed to mimic and even beat Versailles in splendour but currently was still unfinished but the Empress had moved in anyway. Huge tall windows looked over the Neva to the back and to the front was the large palace square. Walls that weren't painted or plastered were lined with sheets of marble or mirrors.

Outside the winter night was descending and snow was falling but no one noticed as they were greeting each other and discussing amongst themselves if they should keep their cloaks on in the smaller unheated salons where they could sit and gossip or play cards. Others quietly discussed whether their Empress would appear in either men's attire or a dress.

There was no announcement of guests so as not to spoil the fun of trying to identify the party goers. There were a few stares at Viktor's dog and at him as well because of his pale hair which was made all the more striking by the fact he was wearing a dark purple waistcoat and coat edged in silver which was a little small for him, and a mask to match. They stepped out of his way as he was led further into the room by Tamara. He tried not to cling too tightly to his sister's arm but he could feel eyes on him even if he couldn't see them. He could hear whispers as well though couldn't discern what was being said. Tamara leant in and said in his ear, "it's all right, you are doing great."

"What is going on? Tell me."

"Well…" Tamara got no further as she was distracted by a friend who had recognised her. Viktor froze when he felt her leave his side. Borya drew closer to him as he sensed his owner's distress. He put his hand on the dog's head and it responded by pressing its head into his hand.

He felt a new presence behind him and cautiously turned as he asked, "who's there?"

"Is that you Viktor Tverdislavich?" Nastasia was surprised to see him. Now that he was standing she realised he stood a head taller than herself and he had a nervous twitch to his mouth.

He stood tall, like a soldier, though his hand dug into his dog's fur suggesting nervousness as he asked again, "who am I talking to?"

"Nastasia Balakina." She smiled behind her cream fan that matched her dress and mask, flirting, as she studied the tight hand in the dog's fur and wondered how often he was allow out.

"You visited my rooms with…?" He said, trying to remember. He had re-lived that half hour a few times and had wondered what would have happened if they had found something to talk about.

"Katerina Livovna, my sister." She answered.

"Viktor?" Another voice entered the conversation. Hearing his mother's voice Viktor didn't know whether to be relieved or angry that she had appeared.

The Countess took hold of him, "what are you doing here? Did Tamara bring you? I shouldn't have let you go to hers." She glanced at Nastasia suspiciously. She knew that the young woman's mother was mistress to a Count and would be looking for someone to keep her like her mother. She led her son towards the side of the room and pressed him into a chair, "stay here for the moment."

"I…." He wanted to say he was a man and that he had a right to be here.

"No Viktor." His mother interrupted, "I am your mother and know how to look after you."
He scowled.

"Stay here and one of us will come and get you for dinner and don't speak to that Balakina girl." Amongst her circle of friends they couldn't comprehend why Count Liv Antonovich Kolesov had brought his bastard up with his legitimate children and even why his now deceased wife had allowed it.

"Why?" He frowned.

"Her mother's a whore." Daria surprised herself at her honesty and then swept across the room in search of her husband and daughter.

Nastasia was shocked that the Countess had appeared and taken Viktor away. She hadn't expected her to dominate her son so much. No wonder he had struggled for conversation when she and Katerina had stumbled upon him.

She was brought out of her shock by her sister who asked, "any reason why you are just standing there?" Nastasia turned, "I'm just trying to work out if I really saw it. Do you remember us coming upon Viktor Tverdislavich?"

"Yes."

"Well, he was here until his mother took him away. She wasn't pleased to see him here."

"Where is he now?"
Nastasia stood on her toes to try and peer over the heads, "he's over by the windows. Come on, he's on his own."

"Too late, they are organising the first dance. Do you have a partner?" Katerina looked round as the floor was cleared for a Minuet.

"Yes." Nastasia answered reluctantly as her dance partner appeared beside her, "you?"

"No." Katerina replied as she slipped away before her sister could force her dance partner on her. Just like Nastasia she was curious about Viktor and though it was quite bold for her she crossed to where he sat and shyly asked, "may I sit beside you?"

"It is free." He answered stiffly.

"You may not remember me but my name is Katerina Livovna." She said after she adjusted her skirts to sit down.

"You found me in my rooms?"

"Yes." She answered brightly, "and you are Viktor Tverdislavich?"

"I am." He smiled softly.

He thought her voice soothing and friendly and wanted to get to know her but he was also attracted by the bold forbidden fruit that was Nastasia Balakina. He wouldn't admit it but he was quite liking the fact two young women were suddenly interested in him. These two young women were new to him, a part of an outside world he didn't know much about. They were like sirens calling to him with sweet promises; exotic creatures waiting to be found.

Returning from seeking her family and organising a quiet place for Viktor to eat so she was not embarrassed Daria was surprised to find him talking to a young woman. She frowned at first thinking it was the Balakina girl but was relieved when the young lady looked up and she recognised her as Katerina Livovna. She still felt a little wary, her protectiveness for her son too strong to relinquish but seeing him laugh at something his companion said made her forgive her daughter a little.

The two young people looked up as the music paused. The Countess smiled ruefully. The Kolesovs may not be the wealthiest of families but they had influence within the Royal circle. She knew that Katerina Livovna ran the family's home since her mother died. She would make a good wife for her son and for the family. It was even better that they had found each other. She would put the suggestion to Tverdislav to re-open the negotiations that had stalled eighteen years previous.

Daria became apprehensive again when she heard Viktor ask, "have you a dance free?"
He was starting to get carried away by the moment and the chance to display he could be independent. She knew he could dance but it had only been in family classes.

"The one before dinner." Katerina smiled. The smile fell a little as the Countess came and sat next to her son. She watched as the Countess leant in and said quietly to her son, "just the one, otherwise you'll be found out."
Viktor stiffened and pressed his lips together as if trying to control himself from saying something out of turn.

The Count came to support him as Viktor and Katerina stepped on to the dance floor. He gently guided him into place. Between his father and Katerina he got through the dance with only a few muttered complaints from other dancers. He bowed as the music ended. Katerina curtseyed and politely remarked, "I think the eye holes on your mask are too small."
He didn't know whether to laugh or feel frustrated. Stiffly, to hide his mixed emotions, he said, "it was a pleasure to dance with you." He held out a hand.
Tentatively she placed her gloved one in his and he raised it to his lips and kissed the back of it. She blushed.

"Thank you for the dance Viktor Tverdislavich." She said as his father gripped his elbow to lead his son away. Viktor briefly resisted but then with reluctance let his father take him from the room. Tverdislav remarked, "it's time for you to go home."

"Why?" Viktor challenged, "I am not doing anything

wrong."

"You aren't but we can't watch over you properly."

"Mother is embarrassed you mean." Viktor remarked accusingly, "she'd rather I hadn't survived." He managed to throw off his father's grip and marched forward, not even thinking about who might be in front of him. He bumped into someone who protested but let it slide.

The next man didn't appreciate Viktor's stumbling around and knocking into his dance partner who squeaked a protest. He reached out and grabbed Viktor, "hey! You owe the lady an apology. Look where you are going."
Viktor tried to throw the hand off him but it got tighter. The man hissed, "apologise to her. Look at her and apologise." Viktor froze for he didn't know where the lady in question was standing.

He was brought back to the moment by the angry man shaking his arm, "you aren't apologising. I am disappointed in you for your poor manners. I challenge you to a duel."
The lady in question gasped and putting a hand on her companion's arm said, "Ivan, don't be foolish. It was an accident."

"No." Ivan retorted, "duels are about honour in France and that is what I'm going to do." He turned back to Viktor, "take off your mask and look me in the eye."
Emotions were high all round and without thinking Viktor pulled off his mask, "happy? And yes I will fight and it will be with swords."

The woman gasped in horror, covering her mouth. She turned her face away from the ugly mess of silvered scars on Viktor's face. Ivan's eyes widened and then he smirked, thinking he was going to have an easy win from this.

Gravil spotted Viktor talking with Ivan Nikitavich

and though he had no time for his brother-in-law he had even less time for the pompous Ivan Nikitavich who thought he was better than everyone else because he had been sent to France for a few years and not to a Germanic State. The Germans were currently out of favour because of Empress Anna and her German lover. He arrived by Viktor's side as the young man pulled off his mask. He'd never seen the mask off him though Tamara had described the scarring to him. It didn't horrify him as much as he thought it would. He had seen war do just as much damage to soldiers, some now begging on the streets after being discharged from the army which was currently fighting the Prussians. He put a hand on Viktor's shoulder and said, "you don't have to go through with this."
Viktor turned, recognising Gravil's voice, "yes I do. I have to show them all that I am a man."
Gravil was silent a moment as he looked between Viktor and Ivan. He knew Viktor was a capable swordsman and would be able to hold his own. Finally he nodded, "fine. I'll be your second."
    "What on earth is going on here?!" Tverdislav arrived, "Viktor get your mask back on before your mother sees."
Gravil turned to Ivan Nikitavich, "give me a time and a place and we will be there."
Tverdislav frowned as he glanced between the three young men, "duels are not Russian. He's not doing this."
    "Yes I am." Viktor said fiercely.
Tverdislav turned his son round and with hands on both shoulders looked him in the one eye that was trying to focus on him. He searched his son's face for any reason to try and convince him not to go ahead but he couldn't. He nodded, "fine. We won't tell your mother."
He turned to Gravil, "I will be there as well. Let me know where and when."
    "Yes sir."

Back to his son he said, "now, lets get you out of here before you mother finds you." He held his son's arm tighter this time as he slipped the mask back on.

Viktor was led away but he stopped as he heard Ivan Nikitavich say behind him, "*Ootebya nyet yayeesav. They are all swivelled up.*"

Viktor's head snapped round. He broke away again, aiming towards where Ivan's voice had come from and swung a fist. Ivan stepped sideways and Viktor fell forward, the momentum of his swing unbalancing him and sending him to the floor with a crash. Only a few people turned, used to people getting too drunk, especially those who remembered their Empress' father, Tsar Peter.

Tverdislav quickly hauled his son to his feet and hissed in his ear, "enough now! You are now making a fool of yourself and our name."

He dragged Viktor from the room, giving him no chance to say anything as he stumbled on his feet to try and stay upright.

Viktor wanted to say so much to his father but knew if he tried saying anything it would just come out angry. He craved the attention of his father but as a man and not as a boy. He knew his parents and sisters were only concerned for his welfare but he still couldn't stop hating them. They wanted to spare him the humiliation and stares but it meant he was always alone.

Nastasia watched from behind her fan with wide eyes as Viktor stood up to Ivan Nikitavich. She saw the reaction of Ivan's companion to Viktor taking off his mask but couldn't see why as his back was too her. For the moment it distracted her from her anger with both the Countess and her half sister. With the Countess Daria Ivanova it was because she had interfered. With Katerina it was seeing her dancing with Viktor. She couldn't believe how neatly Katerina had caught Viktor's attention. She certainly wasn't going to let that happen again. She was going to ensure she witnessed the dual, somehow. It wouldn't be long before her mother would hear as she somehow got all the gossip, sometimes before everyone else heard about it.

CHAPTER 4

There was a mist from the swamps of the estuary of the Neva River as the small group gathered in a wooded area of Pattisaan Island. The island was situated between the Malaya Neva River and the Zhdanovka River, the grounds of one of Tsar Peter's half abandoned pleasure gardens.

The two groups of three men nodded at each other even as they pulled their fur collared coats and cloaks closer around them against the damp chilly morning air. Further back was Nastasia in plain clothes to try and blend in with the leafless trees. Her mother's contacts had worked for her.

She hid behind a tree as the six men stood talking. She recognised Viktor with the hint of his unusual hair peeking out from under his fur hat. His hand nervously rubbed the pommel of his rapier at his side. One of Ivan Nikitavich's companions spoke with a few gestures as he organised everyone.

Viktor couldn't help shivering as he took off his overcoat and held it out for his father to take. His father had been quiet on the boat across and he wished he could see how he was feeling. He hadn't sensed anything different as he had been helped out of the boat and through the overgrown grounds.

He listened as the voices rose and fell in agitation and then a new voice spoke up, "let's get on with this. It's too cold to stay out here. Ivan you get into place since your opponent seems to be wearing a mask." There was a sneer in the tone of voice and Viktor frowned.

Viktor pulled his rapier out, the hilt and handguard of a simple design so his hand didn't get entangled in it, and

said, "let's get on with this."
He cocked his head slightly as he heard a sword being unsheathed between the footsteps of everyone else retreating a short distance away. He calmed his breath, only a small amount of steam rising from his exhalation. He tightened his grip to remember the weight of his sword before loosening it as he had been taught. If he held it too tight he didn't have the control he needed. He knew he wouldn't be getting the tap that his tutor and father gave him.

Ivan Nikitavich smirked. This was going to be too easy. He didn't move from the spot, waiting for Viktor to lurch forward and make a fool of himself again. What he didn't realise was that his feet were shifting in impatience giving his position away on the frosty ground

Viktor waited. He felt sure Ivan Nikitavich would attack first thinking it would be an easy win against a blind man. The shifting feet became an actual firm step forward. He lifted his rapier as he heard the swish of metal in the air and he felt the jar of metal on metal.

There was a screech as the blades scrapped together before parting. Viktor lunged forward in the hope of cutting flesh. He stumbled and heard a harsh laugh. Rightening himself he glared behind his mask in the direction of his opponent. He was being made to feel a fool and knew he was better than that.

He ripped off his mask and squinted as the morning light hit his one good eye. As it adjusted to the light the shapes began to appear. Now he could discern the hazy shape of Ivan Nikitavich. Now he could actually use his fencing skills. He didn't see the grimace Ivan Nikitavich made at his disfigured and scarred face.

Ivan Nikitavich's few seconds of being distracted by the scarring gave Viktor a moment to go on the attack. He stepped in with a swipe and caught Ivan's sleeve. Ivan looked down at the new hole in his shirt and back at Viktor.

The sword fight began now as they took it in turns defending and attacking. Ivan tried to push Viktor over the edge and use more of the space around them but it wasn't happening. Viktor was managing to keep overall control of the duel and Gravil couldn't help being impressed.

Both men, breathing heavily, paused. Tverdislav stepped in between them with hands raised, "that's enough. Sir, have you had your honour defended?"
Ivan looked at the son and then back at the father. He nodded. He held out a hand and his friend handed over his coat and overcoat. He walked away without a word, his two friends hurrying to catch up.

Viktor asked, "is that it?"
"That's it. Satisfied?" Tverdislav remarked sternly, "now, we don't tell your mother about this. She would have you locked up." A smile twitched on his mouth. He was feeling proud of his son. Perhaps he should step between mother and son more to ensure he could have more of a life.
Viktor smiled as Garvil handed him his mask to put back in place. Garvil commented, "I didn't know you were that good!"
Viktor shrugged, "I haven't got much else to do."

Nastasia hid further behind her tree as the three men walked past as they returned to the dock to cross the Zhdanovka River back to the city. She smiled to herself. Viktor was turning into someone to be interested in. Could she make herself attractive enough to the family?

Viktor was on a high after the duel. He felt like a man. Gravil and Viktor excitedly told Tamara about it. She just smiled and nodded as two of the important men in her life seemed to be bonding. They re-enacted the duel, watered wine being spilt on the floor and on their clothes, until Gravil had to leave to visit his barracks.

Gravil left brother and sister in Tamara's small sitting room, Borya lying in front of the ceramic tiled stove. An hour later they heard the front door open and close. Viktor asked, "expecting anyone?"

"No." Tamara was halfway to her feet when the door swung open to reveal their mother not looking particularly happy. Before either of them could say anything their mother exclaimed, "how dare you?! How dare you risk your life for something so foolish as a duel." She turned to her daughter, "I let him come here thinking he would be safe and instead you took him to a ball at the palace and then you didn't try to stop him from getting into a fight." She crossed the room and pulled Viktor to his feet as she continued, "Viktor, you are coming home."

Viktor winced as her fingers dug into his arm. He struggled to get free from her tight grip as she pulled him from the room, out the front door and on to the landing of the apartment building. He exclaimed, "you can't keep me locked up like a child in a nursery. I'm a grown man."

"You can't look after yourself. You need me."

"I don't! Let me be an adult and prove that I am capable."

"But you can't see." She stopped and looked at him. He couldn't see the disgust on her face as she remembered what was hidden by his mask.

She wanted her little boy back, the one before the disfigurement. She didn't want the sight of him everyday reminding her of what could have been. He had survived thanks be to God but he could so easily haven't and now their spare had died and he could have died at the duel! She glanced at the stairs and then back at her son. His feet were close to the edge of the top step and he didn't know it.

She tugged at his arm, causing him to stagger and then he was falling. She let go of his arm as a hand flayed outwards, reaching for anything. He brushed the edge of her skirt as he began rolling down the stairs. He let out a shout of alarm as Borya barked his own alarm.

Tamara ran out on to the landing, "what happened?" Her mother turned to her, gesturing down the stairs, "see!" Tamara looked down the stairs to Viktor lying at the bottom of them with Borya whining and nudging his hand. Her breath caught in her throat and it was only released as she saw her brother move.

Her mother exclaimed, "I told you he needed looking after. He will always need looking after."

Tamara turned to stare at her mother, mouth dropping open. She wanted to protest but couldn't find the words. Her mother raised an eyebrow as if daring her daughter to challenge her.

When Tamara remained silent Daria turned with a swish of her skirts with a smirk of triumph. She exclaimed, "no! Viktor! He's dead!"

Tamara didn't believe it, but Koplev hesitated at his mistress' outburst as he appeared.

Koplev pushed past the Countess and hurried down the stairs. He knelt by Viktor, checking for any broken bones, "sir? Are you alright?"

"Out of the way Koplev. Go fetch the doctor and I'm taking him home." The Countess decreed as she knelt beside her son. She saw her hand shaking from the realisation of what she had done and quickly hid it from the manservant's sight.

Viktor slowly sat up and put a hand to his head, knocking the mask askew. Daria winced at the sight of the glass eye half hidden by the poorly healed eyelid. Her eyes couldn't help following the scar tissue from the eye and across his nose.

Tamara appeared at the foot of the stairs and their mother looked up, "I will take him home."

"He would be better off here if he is injured." Tamara

protested. Her protests turned to Viktor as she saw him try to get up, "Viktor, stay down, you may have some broken bones."

"I…" He swayed on his knees, "my head hurts." He put his hand to the back of it and felt something warm and wet on his fingers.

"That's it!" Daria's voice shook with real concern now as she realised she had injured her son and the now heir and could have killed him. "you are coming home Viktor. We clearly can not trust Tamara to watch over you properly."

"Stop there mother." Tamara protested, feeling hurt by her mother's accusations, "I have been giving him the space to be a man while all you do is keep him hidden away and treat him like a child. He is a man now. He has to be a man now, for the survival of the family."

"And therefore needs to be even more carefully looked after." Daria frowned at her daughter over Viktor's head, "you have allowed him to become injured. Viktor, say your last words to Tamara as you won't be seeing her again." She needed Viktor under her roof, under control as the negotiations between Count Liv Antonovich and the Medevdevs had been restarted due to how Viktor and Katerina had got along at the masked ball. She didn't need him finding himself now and even by accident revealing his injuries. They needed the dowry Katerina would bring with her.

"What?" He felt sore and tired but was aware enough of what was being said above his head, "that's not fair. It wasn't her fault." Though he wasn't sure how he had slipped on the stairs.

"Don't try to protect her Viktor." The Countess pulled her son to his feet.
He swayed on his feet, "you're treating me like a child and I'm not one anymore."

"Don't be silly. You need to be carefully looked after."

Daria said in a voice that was meant to soothe Viktor but it just agitated him this time, not helped by the pain that was emerging from the fall down the stairs. His head hurt and so did his shoulder.

"Tamara?" He turned his head trying to work out where she was as his mother led him away. Sensing his agitation Borya bumped his head against his master's hand to try and reassure him.

He heard her voice, "I'm sorry."

"No." He made a stand for himself, stopping and forcing his mother to stop, "you can't take Tamara away from me."

"Ssh Viktor. It is God's Will that you obey your parents." He could sense Tamara was close to him. He felt warm hands on his and she said in a whisper with a tense smile, "I will see you again when God wills it."

His face twisted up with pain and fear, "Tamara, I'm sorry."

"You have nothing to be sorry about." She placed a kiss on his cheek, "I'll see you sooner then you know it."

"Don't go." He put a hand on one of her's. He felt it slip away as he felt the chill of cold air as he was led to the family's carriage. He didn't want to get stuck in his rooms on his own again.

CHAPTER 5

A day in bed was all he needed to recover and then he was back in his sitting room by the fire listening to Alla reading monotonously. He shifted with a sigh and then winced as his bruised body protested at the movement. He reached for his glass, knuckles touching it first before downing the fiery vodka that was helping to hide the physical pain as well as drowning out his anger at his mother. Alla looked up, "do you want me to stop?"
She straightened up with hope of escaping her brother. She paused as they heard the front door open and shut and murmured voices. Viktor called out, "Koplev, go find out who the visitors are."
Koplev left the room and then returned, "it is Count Liv Antonovich sir, with his daughter."
"Katerina Livonva?"
"I believe that is her name."
Viktor smiled and commanded, "bring her here."
"You aren't meant to have visitors." Alla protested, "mother said so."
"She's not in this room. You can go report on me if you want." He sneered and then snapped at his servant, "do as I say."

Alla retreated to a corner as Katerina entered behind Koplev. She didn't know how her and Viktor had come to know each other but hoped that it meant someone else would take over reading duties. She nodded at the young woman as she passed her before becoming invisible again with a heavy sigh. She felt like the forgotten child.

Katerina wasn't sure whether to be nervous or excited at seeing Viktor again. She knew her sister wouldn't be happy but she didn't have to know and anyway she was only the daughter of a whore and so didn't deserve such an illustrious marriage. She found herself smirking and surprised herself. As the servant announced her she looked round the room now that it was in daylight. It was a small room but looked larger as there was barely any furniture in it. By the window was a small round table with two chairs tucked under it. By the fireplace was a padded settle and an armed chair with a table beside it. On a carpet in front of the fire lay Viktor's dog. Viktor, in the armed, high back chair, turned his masked face towards the door with a smile.

"You wished to see me?" Katerina asked as she approached, worrying about being in the presence of the young man without a chaperone but her father hadn't objected, just waved her way as he had eyed up the tray of drinks and little rye bread open sandwiches. She felt relieved when she spotted Alla in the corner of the room and gave her a tight smile.

"Yes, please come and sit."
She sat on the edge of the settle and couldn't help staring at Viktor with the mask half hiding his face. How did he see?

"You are light on you feet." He remarked, "and you dance a lot better than I ever will."

"Thank you." She blushed and then asked, "are you well?"

"I am thank you. As I recall, you are sister to Nastasia Balakina?"

"Yes." She answered, uncertain where the conversation was going.

"I would like to meet her again."
She was glad he couldn't see her face as it fell. What was it with Nastasia and her attraction to men? But her voice couldn't quite hide the disappointment, "oh?"

Viktor heard the strained tone and after a moment's careful thought said, "my parents and sister are both out

43

tomorrow so would both of you like to visit?”

“I can only ask.”

“Thank you. Has Koplev brought some tea?” He asked as he heard his servant's footsteps.

“He has.” She answered and was relieved the conversation was moving away from her sister. They were meant to be getting to know each other but he seemed to have no social skills. The conversation was stilted. Would it get any better if they married? She took the glass of tea in its silver holder from Koplev.

“Do you know why you and your father are visiting?” Viktor asked out of curiosity as Koplev guided his hand to his own glass of black tea.

“I think there are discussions on a marriage between us.”

“And what do you think of that?”

Katerina blushed, “after our conversation at the ball I wouldn't object. You?”

“If it is God’s Will, so be it.”

“Take off that mask and let me see your face.”

He stiffened, “I can't.”

“Why not?” She asked with concern.

He frowned behind his mask, “I think you should go.”

It came to her then, “you can't see can you?”

He turned his head as he remarked bitterly, “just go.”

Katerina was taken by surprise. He was suddenly coming across as vulnerable and all she wanted to do was hold him. She reached out and tried to touch his hand, “I won't tell anyone Viktor.”

He didn't answer and she looked to Koplev for help but he stared stonily at her. She stood, “well, I hope to see you again soon.”

He didn't move and quietly she left, Alla’s wide eyes on her.

Alla turned to her brother after Katerina left the room. She wanted to give him a huge hug. His simple life was about to get complicated and she could see he wasn't prepared for it. She hoped Katerina wouldn't tell anyone what she had worked out. He didn't deserve to be gossiped about. Silently she stood and left the room, leaving Viktor facing the fire, with no idea what he was thinking. She wasn't bold enough to ask him that.

Katerina was relieved to get home but didn't expect to be pounced on by Nastasia who dragged her to their shared sitting room. Nastasia demanded before Katerina had even sat down, "did you see him?"

"Who?"

In exasperation and with a roll of her eyes Nastasia said, "Viktor?"

"Yes." Katerina reluctantly answered. Why was Nastasia so interested in him? Did she know something that she didn't?

She found herself wanting to keep Viktor for herself. Looking at her half sister she thought she would be too demanding for Viktor. What she thought Viktor needed was a caring wife and a quiet home and not a whore. She surprised herself that she was even thinking that thought.

"Well? Did he ask after me?"

Reluctantly Katerina answered, "yes. We are both invited over tomorrow."

Nastasia eyed her half sister and asked with suspicion, "you are attracted to him?"

"No." Katerina answered half heartedly and demanded, "why are you interested in him?"

"Because… Because…" She couldn't reveal what she had witnessed to Katerina, "because… I saw him first. It was my idea to go exploring and we found him. If it wasn't for me you would never have met."

"This isn't a competition you know. Even if I am going to be the winner."

Nastasia frowned, "what do you mean?"

"Father is engaged in negotiations with them and anyway you wouldn't want him."

"You found out what's wrong with him? What's behind the mask?"

Katerina pressed her lips together. Yes she liked to gossip but felt revealing Viktor's disability would be discourteous to him.

"Well?" Nastasia pressed Katerina shook her head.

Nastasia crossed her arms, "fine but I will find out somehow." Her expression changed then as she realised their relationship was changing as both were now keeping secrets from the other. She felt a little sad.

Nastasia dressed to impress. She wore an ivory white dress pulled low as instructed by her mother with a necklace of amber. She was determined to outshine her sister. She couldn't explain why she was so determined to attract Viktor. Was it because she sensed the same confused lost soul in him that she felt in herself? She knew she was only half accepted in society because of her beauty and her father. If it wasn't for him she would just be a pretty whore in a brothel and that frightened her. With a marriage she would be more secure, and safe from any ridicule.

Katerina was startled but said nothing as she knew Viktor was not going to care for appearances. She saw Koplev raise an eyebrow but pretended she hadn't seen it. He announced, "Miss Katerina Livonva and Miss Nastasia Balakina."

Viktor smiled and stood, determined to show he was a gentleman. He kept a hand on the back of the chair, "welcome and thank you for coming. Please, come and join me by the fire and Koplev will serve us tea."

He heard footsteps approach and returned to his seat, "Katerina, will you always walk around with a whisper?

How will I know if you are in the room or not when we are married?"

"Married?" Katerina asked in astonishment.

"My father told me last night. Have you not been spoken to by yours?"

"No." Katerina answered as she saw hope disappear from Nastasia's confident composure.

"Oh, I'm sorry."

"That's all right."

"Miss Balakina..."

"Please call me Nastasia." Nastasia interrupted and watched his head turn towards her. She smiled seductively at him but she saw no reaction.

"Nastasia, I must apologise for my mother at the ball where we bumped into each other. She is quite protective of me."

"Like any mother should be if you are now the only heir. I have not seen you at a ball before. Have you been away?" Nastasia politely enquired while fighting the urge to ask about the mask and to comment on the duel she had witnessed. She wanted to tell him how impressed she had been.

"It was my first. You could say I have been away." Viktor carefully replied.

Katerina looked between the two of them. Just by his posture she could see Viktor was interested in her half sister but she didn't know why considering they had barely spoken. Looking at Nastasia she wondered if she had worked out that Viktor was blind.

Nastasia was going on, "are you going to the afternoon party happening at the Golitsyns' tomorrow? It's mainly people of our age."

"No. I was unaware of it."

"He may not have got an invite. His family are in a different circle." Katerina came to Viktor's rescue.

He frowned at her having jumped into the conversation. He hadn't needed to be helped.

"Oh?" Nastasia was surprised.

"Even if I had I probably wouldn't go."

"Why ever not? You are back from wherever you have been and now you should be getting yourself known."

"I am recovering from an illness still." He carefully said with a stiffness in his tone that told he knew he was lying. Realising she was beginning to lose him she smiled, "I apologise. You don't look ill so that could fool anyone." He smiled shyly at the compliment, "thank you. Are you both going tomorrow?"

Nastasia looked slyly at her half-sister before saying, "only my sister. Sadly I have not been invited."

She saw him become alert, "perhaps you would like to come here then since neither of us are invited?"

Katerina stared in disbelief at Nastasia as up and till now she had been looking forward to the Golitsyns' party even if she was attending as her companion. She could see that Nastasia was like a maggot in an apple, in a sweet apple. She knew what Nastasia was like with young men and she had broken a few hearts along the way and she didn't want to see it happen to Viktor. He came across too innocence and she knew Nastasia could see that. Katerina wanted to bewitch a man for once and especially the one who was going to be her husband.

She got to her feet, surprising the other two. Nastasia asked with concern, "Kate? Are you alright?"

"I… Nastasia, we should go, I don't feel well." The sooner she got Nastasia away the better.

"Sit awhile and have some more tea Katerina, let it pass over." Viktor suggested, "I have such moments, you just need to sit quietly."

"I… I couldn't stay and burden you but thank you."

"We've only just arrived." Nastasia pouted.

"Please." Katerina stared at her half-sister and hoped her pained look was convincing.

"Oh… umm, yes. Thank you for inviting us."

"Do come tomorrow Nastasia. I'm sure we can find something to do." Viktor remarked hopefully.

"Of course I will." Nastasia smiled and glanced at her sister who looked at her through narrowed eyes.

"I hope you will feel better soon." He stood up out of courtesy and held out a hand to where he thought Katerina was.

She was about to put her hand in his when Nastasia pushed her out of the way and put her own hand in his. He couldn't see what was happening and Katerina realised that Nastasia did know that Viktor couldn't see and hadn't said so and was already using it to her advantage.

Oblivious to the power shuffle between the two sisters he lifted the hand to his lips and kissed the back of it, "you are wearing a different scent. It's too heavy for you. You should stick with the other one."
Nastasia nudged Katerina who reluctantly said, "I will keep that in mind."

"Do not feel obliged to, it was a mere suggestion."

"Thank you for today." Katerina bent down and kissed him on his cheek. Not to be out done Nastasia did the same.

CHAPTER 6

Nastasia wasn't sure how best to present herself to Viktor. Should she be her usual bold self or should she be meeker like Katerina? What personality attracted Viktor? He seemed to have been attracted to both of them at the last meeting. She needed him attracted to only her. She had asked around and no one knew much about him. They could all talk about his dead brother with little sighs but most didn't even know he had had a brother, not even her mother who was the best at having the most interesting and obscure gossip.

The impression she had of him was he was ready to rebel and that she could help with. She was up for some fun while Katerina played at being a socialite before going from one role as housekeeper for her father to the next role as nursemaid to her husband. That was the impression Katerina gave anyway.

Katerina would be at home getting ready for the afternoon party and now she could get Viktor all to herself. Nastasia pushed back the fur lined hood of her cloak as she tugged on the bell pull.

The door opened and the footman stared at her. She flashed him a smile. His face softened a little, "yes?"

"I am here to see Viktor Tverdislavich."

"He doesn't receive anyone."

She frowned, "he invited me."

"He's busy."

"He invited me."

"He wouldn't have."

She peered round the footman and spotted Koplev. She called out, "Koplev!"

Koplev turned and sighed before ordering, "let her in. She was invited over."

The footman sulkily stepped to one side while at the same time glancing at her bosom.

"Thank you Koplev. Is Viktor upstairs?"

He shook his head, "this way."

She was led to the small ballroom. She was left standing in the doorway, her damp cloak in her arms. In the room there was a table with several swords laid on it. Viktor and another man stood before it quietly talking before Viktor reached for one.

She found herself chewing her bottom lip in anticipation at seeing his whole face but he didn't turn her way. Instead, she had to satisfy herself with just watching him practicing his sword skills.

She watched as they paused, as his teacher adjusted the position of a hand, of the rapier with its cup shaped hilt. They talked to each other more like mentor and mentee than teacher and student. Now she understood how he had held his own at the duel.

Her breath caught in her throat as the lesson ended and he lifted the edge of his shirt to wipe sweat from his face and he turned to reveal a well toned chest. She found herself wanting to see more.

She took a step back as she thought she was about to be caught staring and intruding. She bumped into Koplev who grunted. She spun round, "oh, sorry."

"Come with me."

She was led upstairs to Viktor's sitting room.

"Wait here."

"But he is downstairs."

"Wait here."

She heard footsteps in the next door room and a murmur of voices, Koplev's stern one and Viktor's. She approached the open door and peered into the darkened room. Viktor had stripped down to his breeches, exposing more than his chest. His arms looked like they were all muscle as well as his back as he bent over the bowl of water to wash. She bit her lip again, what was hidden behind that mask?

Koplev handed him a linen towel and he dried his face and let his servant tie on a mask. Nastasia retreated to the settle and placed her cloak over the back of it. She perched on the edge nervous that she might have been caught watching.

Viktor entered and headed straight for his chair at the table in the window. He slouched in it. She tried not to laugh, covering her mouth, as she realised he was trying to be cocky. He asked, "well?"

"You knew?" She was taken by surprise.

"Of course. I told Koplev to take you to the room." He smirked and she tried not to laugh again. He was like a little boy trying to act like an adult. Then she remembered how he was topless and that he was all man behind the almost immature front he was currently presenting. She replied with honesty, "you are very good. Have you always practiced?"

"Of course." He grinned, pleased at her answer as he leant on the table his hand creeping across to find the glass of wine he knew Koplev would have left for him. Finding it he brought it up to his mouth and downed it before wiping the back of his hand across his mouth.

The laugh escaped this time. He frowned behind his mask, "what?"

"This is all just bravo isn't it?" She laughed again.

"What do you mean? This is me."

"No sir, it is not. What you were like around your teacher, that was you. This," she waved her hand at his body, "this is you trying too hard."

He sat up, "oh."

"You don't get out much do you?"

He shook his head, "not till recently." He was thoughtful for a moment, "why don't you tell me how to be a better man then."

"That I can do." She smiled. She stood, "now I must go, don't want people talking do we?"
She watched the smile grow on his face and then fall away, "but you haven't been here long. We have barely spoken."

"I'm sorry. I had to check you were sincere."

There was a sharp intake of breath from Viktor as he felt her breath on his ear. How had she crossed the room to him so quickly or had he just been distracted? He recognised the musky scent with hints of spices within it and exclaimed, "it was you!"

"Can't let my sister have all the fun can we?"
He just nodded. He held out a hand and she put one of hers in it. He lifted it to his lips and they probably remained there longer than polite society would approve of. But let him, it wasn't like he was going to have anything else to do all day. Let him have something to remember her by. Gently she pulled her hand free, "aren't you daring."
He softly moaned, "don't go."

She stepped away, now afraid. She had never seen someone fall for her charms so quickly. She gulped and then said, "I'll come back in a day or two."

"Please."
She had the sense of a puppy dog expression behind his mask. Before she sat down again she grabbed her cloak and fled the room.

Viktor stood as he heard the door slam shut. He stared blindly in the direction of the door and muttered, "idiot, idiot, idiot."
He turned and swept the table with his hand sending the glass carafe to the floor. She had laughed at him! How could anyone want a man like him? He tore off his mask

and threw it across the room and sank to the floor. He probably driven her away before he had even gotten to know her.

Nastasia slammed the front door of her mother's apartment shut and stayed leaning against it. She knew what others thought of her, that she was a heartbreaker. She didn't want to be that with Viktor. She was scared for herself, for him. She thought that his social seclusion had caused him to latch on to the first young women to pay him any attention. Her mother would tell her to run with it, lure him in and then spit him back out once she was done. Would she go back? She probably shouldn't but a part of her wanted to get to know Viktor better. There was something in him crying to get out with the help of the right person and could she be that person?

CHAPTER 7

Following her mother's advice she lured, complimented and teased Viktor. It had started with conversations, with light touching as she helped herself to the honey sweetened gingerbread that Koplev had placed on Viktor's table. She would lean in so he could catch her perfume. It always caused him to catch his breath which made her giggle. She found that after their first few stilted conversations the talk began to flow. She read to him and told him all the gossip and he lapped it up.

Viktor found this was a different sort of attention compared to his mother's overbearing attention or Alla's reluctance. This was focused on him as a man. What Nastasia saw in him he didn't know but he was enjoying it. At her touches he felt his body come alive in new ways which was better than the high energy he got from fencing.

She found herself as hungry for his touch as he was for hers. She accidently leant in too close to him and he turned his head, his lips brushing against her cheek and then her lips. Startled, she leant away, eyes wide, trying to work out what to do.

"What's wrong?" His hand reached for her's.
She looked at him, wondering if he realised what had happened.

He knew she was close, so close that he could feel the heat radiating from her where he had accidently brushed her with his lips. He asked the question and heard her take a sharp breath. He remembered how he had seen a maid and stable groom kiss in the stables before he had been blinded and wondered if he should dare.

He had an idea of where her head was and lifted his hands. Finding her head he held it, long fingers getting tangled in her hair. He kissed her tentatively at first and when she didn't try to push him away he pressed his lips harder against hers.

She pushed him away, panting. She was surprised by how good it had been but she felt guilty as well. This was the man who was going to be her half sister's husband.

Her mother was home when she went there after that kiss, seeking advice. Her mother was a plump woman who was still attractive all these years later even with Nastasia's unplanned conception. After she had given birth she was more careful about getting pregnant. She doted and ignored her daughter in equal measure and had been greatly relieved when Liv Antonovich had taken her in to be taught with his other daughter.

She looked up from her book and eyed her daughter with suspicion, "what has happened with your new love interest? There is something different about you. Are you glowing?"

Nastasia sank into a seat, "he kissed me."

"Good."

"But he is going to marry Katerina."

Her mother shrugged, "and the problem is? You can carry on having fun while she is stuck in a loveless marriage."

"This is different." She felt a connection she had never felt with all the others she had flirted with. He was inexperienced in the world of sophisticated flirting but that didn't matter. His approach was almost instinctive, reacting to her through other senses.

"You need to test it then? Test whether he wants you. You know the drill."

"Yes mother."

"And if this means a more secure life for you then screw your sister over." Her mother smirked.

"But what would happen between you and papa?"

Her mother shrugged, "probably a few weeks of peace

before he comes crawling back. He's too content with me
to go through the effort of finding another mistress. I won't
tell if you don't." She raised an eyebrow.
Nastasia nodded.

"You have the biggest prize. Make sure you are giving
yourself to the right person." Her mother crossed the room
and sat beside her daughter. She took her head in her hands
and stared into her face, "you only lose your true virginity
once."

"If papa is the one for you, why did you not marry him
when Katerina's mama died?"

"Because we were happy as we were."

"I want to be the wife."

"You are too young to want that. Remember, you and me,
we aren't restricted to social norms. We can be what we
want to be, no arranged marriages for us.

"But I want that for me."

"Then like a fish you'll have to reel him in and catch him
in your net and not let him fall out otherwise Katerina will
have him."

She watched from the back of the church, her
thoughts filled with hunger for Viktor and jealousy because
of her sister. Just days previous Katerina had heard she'd
been seeing Viktor alone and their sisterhood and
friendship had burnt to ashes. Now she felt all alone. She
couldn't reveal herself to Viktor as just two days previous
she had told him she was going on a short pilgrimage just
like the Empress liked too.

Tears silently slid down her cheeks for no reason
she could explain as the rings and the couple were blessed.
She wanted to be the one standing with Viktor but couldn't
fully understand why. She didn't think it was love. This
wasn't one of her mother's books.

This forced distance was hard on her and she hoped

it was hard on Viktor. He had reluctantly accepted her explanation but his hand on hers suggested otherwise. She had looked up but the damn mask hid his face and she couldn't tell if he wanted her or just enjoyed the social interaction. If it was just the conversation he was welcome to Katerina and she would become a nun. She surprised herself with that thought.

Before any of the two families could see her she slipped out of the church and returned to her mother's apartment.

At the church Katerina was trying not to be too smug that she had got one over her half sister. She was glad that Nastasia wasn't there. She couldn't believe that her half sister had been seeing her betrothed behind her back. If she was of a more malicious character she would have started a rumour to tarnish her, but though she had shut her out she couldn't find it in her to do it. There were too many good times together to remember. Without her life would have been lonely as her three brothers were off doing other things and her mother had died. The attention was now on her. She would have loved to have had a ball to celebrate the engagement but that wasn't to be. Both families had agreed to just have a large dinner. She looked at Viktor standing opposite her and wondered whether he was the best option for her. She enjoyed a party and would married life with him curtail that?

The black cassocked priest, rings in his fist, made the sign of the cross above her head, "the servant of God, Viktor Tverdislavich Medvedev is betrothed to the maid of God, Katerina Livovna Kolesov; in the name of the Father, of the Son and of the Holy Spirit."
She took a ring from his hand and placed it in Viktor's so he could place it on the third finger of her right hand which she held out for him. She felt his fingers trembling and

realised he was as nervous as she was inside.

There was a sigh of relief from the families as she put a ring on Viktor's right hand. The deed was done and now they could plan for the wedding in a few months' time. All of them thought that the young couple were a good match especially when they were sat together at the dinner after the blessing and an emerald ring been given as a gift from the groom to be. The Countess, with trepidation, allowed Katerina to help Viktor.

Viktor was relieved when the day was over. He was tired from both the day where every move he had made had to be careful and from several nights of erratic sleep. All he had been thinking about was Nastasia, wondering what she was doing. Was she thinking about him? How could he tell her how much he needed her? Was this infatuation or love or the fact someone had given him attention that had felt natural not forced? It was all so confusing.

He got the chance the day after the betrothal when he and his father sparred under the critical eye of their fencing tutor. Since the duel his relations with his father had changed for the better. As they fenced now they talked and laughed as father and son, not acting like strangers.

Tverdislav was pleasantly surprised at the change in his son. The duel and the two young ladies had done wonders to Viktor and his confidence. He liked both sisters even though his wife disliked Nastasia for some reason he couldn't understand.

Today Viktor was enjoying feeling the cool air of the room on his face. His one eye could just discern where his father stood in the room against the light of a clear late winter sky outside. They advanced, clashed and retreated. There was a grunt from the fencing tutor who walked around them with his arms crossed. They advanced on each other again and sparred, each moving back and forth and

around each other. Viktor broke through his father's defence and Tverdislav surrendered with a smile, "well done."
There was a "hmpfh." from their fencing tutor and both father and son snorted in laughter. That grunt was the closest they were going to get for praise from the man today.
"Time is up." The man bowed at the Count before leaving.
As Koplev took the rapiers from father and son Viktor asked cautiously, "what would you get a lady?"
"A gift for Katerina?" Tverdislav asked with a knowing look.
"No." Viktor carefully replied.
"Oh? Who then?"
"Her sister."
"Nastasia Balakina?"
Viktor gulped nervously as he wasn't sure how his father would react to the name, "yes."
Tverdislav wasn't sure what to make of that for a moment but then chuckled to himself, his son had become a man. He remembered the times his own father had sent him to one of the maids on the estate to learn how to be a man.
He took hold of his son and led him to a window seat. They sat in it as Tverdislav advised, "enjoy these next two months but out of respect for your bride to be keep it discreet."
"Yes sir."
Tverdislav studied his son's face. He could see him struggling with his emotions. He smiled again, "get her a bracelet."
"You hear that Koplev?" Viktor asked, "find one for me, a nice one."
"Yes sir. Any gemstones in particular?"
Viktor looked to his father who replied, "garnets." He

beckoned Koplev to him. He glanced at his son before quietly saying, "when she next comes bring her to me first."

"Yes sir." Koplev bowed his head.

CHAPTER 8

Nastasia looked at the note that had been sent to her and felt thrilled and nervous. She went to her mother. Valentina Balakina looked up from her book, "what is it?"

"Viktor Tverdislavich has sent me a message asking after me."

"Are you back from your journey then?" Her mother smiled.

Nastasia shrugged. This was her mother's idea. Her mother's smile dropped and her tone changed, "do you want to become a pauper, selling yourself for a pittance?"

"No."

"It's too late to try for his wife. How much do you want him?" She sat up and shifted to the edge of the settle she was on and looked at her daughter, her beautiful daughter, standing before her, who had yet to realise she would only be good for one thing and if she really did marry it would be someone beneath her. Her illegitimate status meant no one of respectability and wealth would want to marry her.

Nastasia pressed her lips together. She was rapidly descending into her mother's world but she wanted Viktor. It was too complicated to explain. It had been hard to stay away. She'd only known him for a little over a month but felt he was the man for her. Forever, she wasn't sure, but the word soulmate came into her thoughts. She didn't dare speak and reveal her thoughts so nodded.

"If he wants you, you are going to have to give him more than just kisses now." Valentina informed her daughter, "all men are only after one thing. Sex. Just make sure he pays you in gifts and then keep them for when you might need the money."

"And if I don't want to?"

"You have no choice." Her mother said sternly.

Nastasia's eyes widened.

"Oh, I had that desire once, but I accepted my place in society a long time ago. They accept you for your blood and respect your skills in the bedchamber, but they desire to ignore you as much as they can. Wives don't want to image their husbands needing a bed that's warmer than their own and don't want it rubbed in their faces. Katerina will soon become the same. That friendship is now over." Valentina remarked harshly, "now come and sit beside me. I need to tell you what you need to do."

"I don't want to hear this." Nastasia protested.

"Come here." Her mother ordered and patted the cushion beside her.

Nastasia reluctantly sat down beside her mother.

Her mother's voice became more gently, "the important thing is that you are relaxed. It will make his entrance easier. They like to be touched on their cocks and to touch your breasts so let him. Now, he's a young man so you shouldn't worry about having to aid in rising. They are quite good at springing up of their own accord. It's older men who struggle then you must coax an erection."

"Mother!" Nastasia blushed though it was not the first time her mother had been blunt.

"At least you know what is going to happen. I have never wanted you to go into the bedroom unprepared. So many young women have no idea and are afraid of sex." Her mother pointed out. "You get to go in and know what you want and enjoy it."

"What if I become pregnant?"

"Then we'll get rid of it."

"What if I don't want to?"

"Then you are a fool! Only a fool or wife would bear child after child. After so many children you won't attract a lover who will keep you as their mistress then?"

"Then why did you have me?"

"I realised too late. You haven't wanted for anything though, have you?"

"No." Nastasia bowed her head.

"Good. Now, I've told you everything you need to know so go and reply to his note, wash, put on your best clothes, smile and go and seduce him." Valentina sat back and returned to her book.

She expected Koplev to take her straight to Viktor so wondered what was going on when she was led before the Count. She shifted uncomfortably as she stood before Viktor's father who sat at his desk.

He briefly glanced up at her before returning to the letter he was writing to the steward on the family estate. He wanted her nervous. He wanted her to know she was here in the house because of him and not Viktor.

With the letter finished he finally looked up and took Nastasia in. He knew of her mother and saw in her daughter what Count Liv Antonovich saw in the mother with her glossy brown hair and large brown eyes. It was a shame his son would not see her physical beauty but he must have sensed something to be attracted to her. He approved of the simple red dress she wore. It was a shame that she was younger than Viktor, probably as inexperienced, but needs must in getting him practiced ahead of him becoming a husband. If Viktor hadn't claimed her he would have been tempted to have her for himself.

She could sense that he was attracted to her and felt even more nervous. Was the father planning to taste her before the son? She cautiously asked, "sir?"

"I wished to speak with you first."

"Yes?" Were her plans about to unravel?

"Viktor is betrothed to Katerina Livovna and that can't be changed. You will never be more than his mistress. Do you understand?"

"Yes sir."

"As long as he remains your *only* lover and you keep him happy you will have a stipend. Do you understand?"
Her eyes widened briefly at the fact she really was going to be a mistress. She nodded her head.

"Do you understand?"

"Yes sir, thank you sir."

"He must not know of this agreement. If he finds out that money will stop and you won't be allow in this house again. You must be discreet. This is the last time you come through the front door. I will not be having you embarrass my wife if you want to keep seeing him. If he gets bored of you then that's it, you will not come pleading, you will simply stop. Am I making myself clear?"
She nodded.

"Good. Koplev please take Miss Balakina to my son." Tverdislav beckoned his secretary over and returned to the papers on his desk.

Koplev silently showed Nastasia into Viktor's suite. Viktor looked up from where he sat at the table by the window, "please come and sit with me."

"Are you well?" She asked as she sat down and spotted the square leather box on the table. She had an inkling of what was in it considering the conversation she had just had with his father.

"I'm glad you have come. It was quiet without you. How was your pilgrimage? Did you find the answers you were seeking?" He asked as he reached out a hand and sought out the box on the table. Finding it he pushed it across the table, "I hope that this will show you how I feel."
She took a deep breath, unsure how she felt about the 'payment' before reaching for the box and opened it. She wasn't sure what to expect but wasn't disappointed with the bracelet of a band of gold with small enamel flowers weaving round and meeting with a larger one with a large

garnet at its centre.

"That can be the first of many if you wish." He remarked, taking the silence as shock.

"Viktor I wasn't expecting this, thank you." She realised that she may not have the ring but she had the man. She hadn't heard of Katerina getting any gifts but then they hadn't spoken.

"I'm glad you like it." He said stiffly making her realise that it was the first time he had given a gift to a woman that wasn't a relative. She knew what would be expected of her now.

She took hold of one of Viktor's hands and drew him to his feet. She bit her bottom lip, feeling nervous about what was about to happen and she was glad he couldn't see it. She led him towards his bedroom. He froze, "where are we going?"

"To your bedroom. That is what we both want isn't it?" He remembered his desire for her and gave her a nod and let himself be led to his bedroom. He pushed Borya away with his foot.

They sat on the edge of his bed, both hesitating. She held on to his hand and drew in a deep breath.

"Perhaps a drink?" He suggested. He needed something to calm his nerves. He knew his brother had been happily having sex with anyone who would willingly lift their skirts for him, including days before his idiotic death. He used to visit and boast about it.

"That would be nice."

She watched him stand and find his way to the end of the bed and then take careful steps to the door. He called out of the door, "Koplev, can you bring some wine."

"Yes sir."

Carefully he returned to the bed with a smile. He sat back down and found her leg and squeezed it through her skirts.

She turned to him and put her hands on his face and

kissed him. He smiled into the kiss and returned it. His hand slid round her waist and back again as he sought out the strings that pulled her bodice tight. He tugged at one end till they became undone, releasing her breasts from their confinement.

Animal instincts took over and he pushed her back on to the bed and moved so he knelt over her. He kissed her hard on the lips, hungry for her. His mouth moved to her neck, savouring her spicy scent which was intoxicating since its absence.

A hand found its way to a breast and she gasped as he squeezed it a little too hard.

"Sorry." He said into her neck.

"Gentler."

There was the faintest of nods as he moved down and buried his face in her cleavage while she reached down and found the buttons of his breeches. She flinched as she found his penis already growing and it pulsed at her touch.

He froze and tried to remember what happened next between the maid and the stable groom, but his mind was filled by the fact Nastasia's hand was on his erection. He didn't want to spoil the moment, but he whispered into her powdered cleavage, "what now?"

Nastasia stared up at the ceiling, taking in the crack on it, as she absorbed what he had said. She lifted her hips and pulled her skirts up out of the way before taking one of his hands. She guided it between her thighs as she whispered, "here."

His fingers explored the folds of her sex and she let out a little gasp as he found the little bump that when she rubbed it aroused her. His fingers slipped into her wet sex. She bit her lip as he pulled a crooked finger out, catching at her insides, teasing her heightened senses. She began to wonder if they should be doing this, was it too soon?

He shuffled up her body, between her legs,

squashing her, his breath tickling her ear. She could feel the tip of his cock bumping against her. She took a deep breath and reached down. They might as well get the awkward first time over with. She guided him in and squeezed her eyes tight shut as he pushed into her tight passage. It hurt but her body responded by making it wetter and easier for Viktor to thrust in and out of her until he came with a groan.

She lay still as he panted in his ear, tears seeping under her eyelashes. Her destiny had been decided for her now. One of her tears must have touched Viktor for he propped himself up, "Nastasia? Why are you crying?"

"I'm alright." She could feel blood and his semen dripping out of her. She turned her head away. He carefully sat up, straddling her as she pressed her legs together. A hand felt its way up her stomach and chest till he found her face and wiped a tear away with a thumb.

The moment ended as Koplev cleared his throat. Nastasia pushed her skirts down in embarrassment while Viktor slipped off the bed and did his breeches up. She watched Koplev place the tray on a table and wondered how much he had seen. Would he be reporting back to the Count? She said, "thank you Koplev."

"Anything else?"

"No." Viktor answered as he sat down on the edge of the bed, "Nastasia are you all right to pour?"

"Of course." She said carefully as she watched Koplev leave.

Koplev headed downstairs when he saw he wasn't going to be needed for a few hours. He smiled to himself and as he sat down at the servants' table to help polish the Medvedevs' boots he remarked, "he's finally a man."

"The Balakina woman?" A maid asked.

Koplev nodded.

"How long do you think it will last? What on earth does she see in him considering she has any number of better-looking men sniffing around her." The footman asked as he put down the boot he had just finished cleaning.

"Don't know but since his Lordship has promised her money, I think she will be around for as long as possible but that might change if the Countess finds out."

"Poor sod but I bet he'll soon get bored now that he has had her. He'll want someone else soon enough."

"He will have someone, Katrina Livovna." Koplev pointed out as he reached for a rag.

"And then he will be the experienced one and in charge." The footman remarked with a sneer at the maid.

"We can be in charge as well, just look at the Tsaritsa." The maid pointed out in protest.

"But she changes her mind and is easily distracted like any other woman." The footman argued back.
The maid scowled at him.

Upstairs Nastasia and Viktor sat on the bed sipping wine and dipping *sushki* in it. Nastasia had slipped out of her main dress and discreetly washed the blood stain with water and now sat against the pillows in her chemise. She studied him out of the corner of her eye as he held the glass in his two hands. With pent up curiosity she asked, "what's under your mask?"
A hand went to it as if he feared she would take it off, "not yet."

"What is it like to not be able to see?"

"Isolating." He sighed as he passed his glass to her, "I can just about discern dark and light. I have no true independence."
She put the two glasses on the table and turned back to Viktor. She lay down on her side, propping her head up with a hand, as she asked, "how do you know where

everything is or what something looks like?"

"By touch."

"How would you know what I look like?" She wondered out loud.

"I can show you." He answered, guessing where this was going even if she hadn't realised. He could feel an erection growing again at the thought of exploring her body, "take off your clothes."

"What if someone comes in?" She wasn't sure whether she wanted to or not. Her virginity was gone and if it was going to be anything like the fumbling sex earlier she didn't want any more sex.

Her life was now set on the path to be a man's plaything and the only good thing was she had got to choose who took her virginity. Maybe if she had more sex with Viktor she might find the pleasure her mother found in it.

"Alla is visiting friends in Moscow and as long as I'm not embarrassing my mother she will pretend I don't exist."

She slipped off the bed and removed her chemise. Goose pimples formed in the chilly air. As she sat on the bed she said, "you too."

He fumbled over the small buttons of his waistcoat and then pulled it off with his shirt.

"Your mask?" She asked again.

"No." He found her naked thigh and felt her tense at his touch.

She lay down on the bed and tried not to look at Viktor and his thin but well toned body, as he straddled her. He murmured, "stay still."

He knelt over her and with his hands began to trace her features. He ran his fingers over her hairline and then down her forehead, over her eyes and nose. They found her plump lips that held a tentative smile. He left a finger there as he leant over to kiss her lips.

From there he followed the curve of her jaw up to an ear and back. From her chin he ran his fingers over her throat. His hands spread across her chest and found her round breasts with their pert nipples. He gave them a squeeze as he leant into her throat and smelt the musky perfume she wore. She giggled as his warm breath touched her chilly skin.

His fingers found the under curve of Nastasia's breasts and then swept over her stomach. He felt sure she was holding her breath as he found her belly button. From there he found the top of her curly haired mound which hid her sex which his erection was pressed against.

She found herself breathing heavier and faster as the light touch of his fingers found her sex. He found the little bump that she had discovered herself a few years back. She held his hand there and showed him how to rub it. She let out a moan and let go of his hand.

He paused and she panted, "don't stop. Keep going."

His thumb kept rubbing it as with the fingers of his other hand he found her wet sex and though it briefly resisted his prying finger it was soon in.

She shifted and moaned again, pushing herself on to his fingers. This was different from when she did it herself. She stopped too soon when on her own but with Viktor she could make him keep going. She squirmed and fought the urge to tell him to stop.

Having a sense of her body now he leant over her and kissed her as she squirmed under his touch. He asked, "is this good?"

"Yes. Please don't stop. Squeeze my breast."

He changed his hand position and found her breast with its hard nipple. The novelty of it had him rubbing it with his thumb. He felt her clench round the finger that was inside her and wanted to feel her round his penis. He asked, "can

I?"

"Yes." She moaned.

This time he didn't need help finding his way in. He found her tight entrance himself and with a firm thrust from his hips he was in, pressing in as far as he could, filling her with his whole length and width. She released a breath she didn't realise she had been holding and it came out as a long satisfied moan. She held him in, wrapping her legs round him, not wanting him to leave her. She wanted to feel him in her. She said, "don't move."
But it was too much for him and she felt him come within her.

He rolled off panting and on a high so high he couldn't explain how he was feeling. He couldn't speak. He reached out for Nastasia's hand. She let him hold it briefly before pulling away.

Her feelings were all confused. She shifted away from him and reached for her chemise. She tried to ignore the blood and semen sticking her thighs together as she pulled on her clothes.

"Nastasia?" Viktor sat up.
She kept her hand away from his as he reached blindly for it, sensing the cooling spot where she had been. He didn't need to know how she was feeling. She slipped on her shoes and left the bedroom. She saw Koplev in the day room and said, "can you show me out?"

"Of course." He gruffly replied.
From the bedroom there was a shout, "Nastasia? Koplev?"

"I will see to him afterwards. What do you want me to say?"

"That I will be back."

"Of course."

"Nastasia?"
She foolishly turned and saw Viktor standing in the doorway naked. The thought 'man-child' came to her and

she tried to start building a wall round her heart. She ordered, "Koplev, show me out."

Nastasia returned to her mother's apartment and ordered a bath. She sat in it having scrubbed herself clean staring into space, thinking, trying to work out what she was feeling. Was it all lust or was there something more? Her mother entered while she wallowed all pink skinned. Nastasia rolled her eyes as she sneered in frustration, "come to tell me that I'm a good whore?"
She saw then that her mother was looking concerned. She wondered whether her mother had ever had the same thoughts she had had. She looked like she was going to hug her. Her mother had decided to play at being a mother. Nastasia looked away.
    "How was it?"
Nastasia tried to work out what her mother would want to hear. Did she tell the truth or tell a lie? She shrugged her shoulders, "it was alright."
    "Only alright?"
    "It was messy the first time..."
    "And?" Valentina asked encouragingly.
    "Am I expected just to lie there?" Nastasia exclaimed. She wasn't ready to speak of the emotions and sensations she had felt from his exploring fingers.
Her mother smiled from where she sat, "yes and no. Here," she produced the book that she had been carrying, "I think you will find this helpful. There is more than one way to have sex and every man has a different preference. Some like to be a man whereas others like the woman to be dominant." She smiled to herself as if she was recalling some past bedroom event. She passed the book to her daughter, "the best thing about being a mistress is you are there for his pleasure and yours if he is that way inclined unlike a wife who is there to create the babies."

"What is this book?"

"A book of dreams. I suggest you look at it when you are alone." Valentina smiled before leaving her daughter staring at the blank cover of the book.

That night Nastasia sat in her bed. She tried to ignore the book. She had briefly glanced in the book earlier and felt a little repulsed. With a sigh she gave up on the book she was reading. The front piece in French read, 'The School of Venus. The ladies delight, reduced into rules of practice'. Her mother had given her a sex manual. She wondered how the church would react if they knew she held it.

She started turning the pages, skimming over the conversation between Frank and Katy, shocked at the crudeness of it. She came to the first plate which showed a dressed couple with the woman bent over with her skirts resting on her back and the man penetrating her from behind. She couldn't help feeling turned on by the image and the ones that followed. And then she recalled Viktor's touch on her skin that had been both tentative and bold.

She found herself wanting more. Her groin tingled. Her body wanted more of the new sensations. One thing she did know was she wanted to be in control if this was to be her life. She would be the one to dictate what happened in bed. The book suggested that a woman could lead the sex by the woman being on top. She smiled to herself and knew what she needed to do. With that decision made all she had to do was wait for Viktor to send a message.

CHAPTER 9

It was another day before Viktor sent an invitation. She made sure she wore her gift if he went seeking it. She was surprised to find him in only his shirt and breeches, slouched in his chair. His hair was damp. There was an air of confidence about him as he had just been doing his sword practice. He spoke, "Nastasia?"

"It is me. How are you?"

"Good, thank you. And you?"
She wondered if their meetings were always going to start so stiffly considering how relaxed they had been lying in bed, "I am well."

"I am glad you came." He held out a hand. He had originally planned to ask her why she had left so abruptly the last time, but now she was here he didn't actually care. Just hearing her voice reassured him that she was here, in his rooms, willingly.

She crossed the room and took his hand and bent down, "I have something to show you."
Behind his mask his eye widened. He let her draw him up and to the bedroom. She didn't want to sit gossiping about people that meant nothing to either of them. If she was going to be Viktor's mistress, she wanted it on her terms. She wasn't going to be some stiff corpse for any man. She hoped Viktor would respond positively.

Once in the bedroom she pushed him on to the bed. He resisted, "what are you doing?"

"I have learnt some things that might help us." She said.
He frowned, "help us? What do you mean? From where?"

"A book. Can we at least try?" She asked.
He wasn't sure but allowed her to do what she wanted since it was still all new to him.

She took off her dress but remained in her chemise

as he shuffled up to be against his headboard. He felt the
mattress move as Nastasia came to straddle across him.

She leant forward and went for his mask. His hand
went up to stop her, "what are you doing?"

"Let me see."

"You don't want to."
Gently she said, "let me."

"But you'll then leave." He whispered with fear, "it is
why I am kept away from everyone."

"Let me." She repeated and took his hand off hers.

He didn't resist but did hold his breath as she
removed his mask. There was silence as she stared at the
scarring and his glass eye. He could feel her thighs tense
round his legs as she tried to decide how she felt.

She felt horrified and sympathetic all at the same
time. Cautiously she reached out to trace a scar and saw
him breath again. She asked, "does it hurt?"

"Sometimes." He whispered, "you are not afraid?"

"No." She lied. She leant in and kissed his scarred
forehead. She saw him tentatively smile and kissed the
smile. She sat up again, "how did it happen?"

"A bear attacked me when I was ten. The scars
embarrassed my mother which is why I wear these masks."

"All the time?"

"Most of the time. When I am fencing I don't wear one. I
can discern shape at least which helps."

"You are very good. That time I saw you practicing
wasn't the first time I've seen you." She admitted. She
stared down at her hands that currently rested on his
stomach and then back up. She saw his one eye trying to
focus on her. Finally she said, "that duel you did, I saw it,
from a distance. How has nothing been said of your….?"
She wasn't sure what to call his scars.

"Because who is going to admit they were nearly beaten
by a blind man?" Viktor scoffed.

76

She shifted as she felt his growing erection through his clothes.

"What's wrong?" He hesitantly asked.

"Nothing." She hesitated. This time was different from the other day. That was about sating themselves. This time she had initiated it but now wasn't so sure. She had seen behind the mask and was trying not to feel repulsed. She was glad she had got to know him before the mask had come off.

"We don't need to rush this."

"No…no…" She was glad he couldn't see her expression. She reminded herself she had wanted him and that she had got there before Katerina. She looked into his face and saw confusion on it. She took a deep breath before pulling his shirt up and undoing his beeches.

His breathing became more rapid as he asked, "what are you doing?"

"Taking control." She said as she ran her hand up the length of his erection and it grew stiffer. She took one of his hands and put it to her chemise covered breast. His thumb rubbed at her nipple making it hard and she straightened her back. She put his other hand on her hip as she adjusted herself. He slipped his hand from her breast to between her thighs where he found her clenching. He found her clit and rubbed at it as she had shown him previously and she began to relax. She lifted herself into him before lowering herself on to his penis, biting her lip as she did.

He let out a moan as his member became enclosed in her tight folds. His free hand held tight to her hip as the other continued to rub at the small bump while she rocked in his lap, panting. She leant in and he felt her breasts close to his face and smelt the perfumed powder she had dusted over them. Impulsively he buried his face between her breasts.

She gasped as she felt herself come, squirming

against his hand trapped between them, taken by surprise at how different it felt from when she touched herself. Viktor came shortly after as he felt her tighten around him. He sat more upright and clung to her as she leant against him and moaned as he came. They remained locked together panting, both wishing it had lasted longer but the excitement of it all had won again. She felt him go limp and slipped off him and he sighed. He had liked her sat in his lap.

She slipped to the edge of the bed and Viktor reached out, "don't go."
She turned to look at him, "I'm not going anywhere. I'm just getting a drink." She spotted his banyan, a lined heavy silk Damascus dressing gown, over the back of a chair and reached for it, "do you want one?"
"Go on."
She felt his eye watching her as she walked into his day room, his banyan dragging along the floor behind her and found a tray with snacks on the window table in the other room.

She was thoughtful as she returned to the bedroom. She and Viktor were only at the beginning of a relationship that could quickly get complicated. What did either of them even want? It had started as friendship for Viktor, she could see that. For her it had been intrigue, one woman upmanship against her half-sister and the hope of an opportunity. That opportunity had changed so why had she come back? Had they jumped into sex too quickly? Did he know this couldn't last?

He sensed her contemplation, "what are you thinking?"
"I…" She paused as she tried to put what she was thinking into words, "have we rushed into this? Is our relationship going to be only about sex?"
"I don't know." He wanted to walk out with her on his

arm but he had Katerina to think about, "what do you want?"

"I don't know."

"I want to be with you."

"Why though? We met, like…. A month ago and now we are tumbling in the sheets."

She looked at him naked on the bed in the most vulnerable state a man could be in and even more so that he was blind but if he had a shashka in his hand she knew he could defend her. He might be blind, but he had survived so that had to be a good thing. Had God wanted them to be together but was testing them? But then why was God allowing Viktor to marry Katerina.

He broke into her thoughts, "I don't know. It feels right, right? You found me so that has to be something. We can make this whatever we want it to be, just you and me. If you just want to sit and read then do so. Alla rarely comes and mother has her own life and probably would prefer my brother to still be alive for the sake of the family. Now, I thought you were bringing drinks."

"I have them here." She laughed and leant over the bed to give him his.

"So… Where did you learn that?"

"Learn what?"

"I thought there was only one way of having sex." She giggled, "my mother gave me a book."

"Anything else in it you've learnt?"

"Maybe." She giggled and blushed.

Conversation turned to her mother and her father. From there it led to Katerina and the fact she and Nastasia had parted ways. Viktor asked, "do you miss her?" Without hesitation she responded, "yes."

She blinked rapidly to fight back tears. She missed being with not just a sister but one of her few real friends. She wondered what Katerina was doing without her and whether she was feeling a little lonely as well. She still saw her father when he visited but she knew she had to stay out of the way as he was there to see her mother, not her. She was just a result of their arrangement, "I'm impulsive and she was always good at restraining me and I made her life more interesting otherwise all she has is the boring work of running our father's household for him."

"I'm glad she doesn't always restrain you." He smiled as he heard the sadness in her voice.

"Thank you." Though she wasn't sure as it was because of him they had stopped talking. To divert the conversation away from herself she asked him about his family.

He spoke angrily of his mother but with pride of his father and adoration of Tamara. He ended, "I know she thinks she is protecting me from whispers and embarrassment, but I have found it more and more restricting especially when all I had to look forward to was my fencing practice but now I also have you." He smiled again.

She didn't say anything for a moment. They were both so new at this and she hoped Viktor wouldn't become too demanding or get bored of her too quickly.

.

CHAPTER 10

It was a week before Nastasia saw Viktor again. When she did respond to his invitation the nervous tension seemed to have gone. There was no longer an urgency to just have sex but she had brought the book with her. After greeting Viktor she raided his bedroom for pillows and blankets. Koplev asked stiffly and suspicion, "do you need any help there?"

"Oh no, but you can get us some snacks and wine." She said as she dropped the pile on the floor in front of the fire. She pushed Borya out of way who growled in protest.

"What are you doing?" Viktor asked as he perched on the edge of his chair.

"Did you ever make a hideaway with your bedding?" She asked with a mischievous smile.

"Probably. I kind of try not to think about before the attack. Why?"

"This is a more grown up version. Come and join me on the floor."
Carefully he got down on hands and knees and found the edge of Nastasia's forming nest. She took his hand and guided him on to it, "you sit there while I adjust everything… Oh Koplev, bring the tray over here and then you can go." She ignored the servant's disapproving look.

Feeling triumphal she sat back on her knees and decreed, "done."
With a giggle she pulled Viktor down to the floor so they lay propped on the pillows. She found her book and felt like a child who had found a naughty book, "I brought the book with me."

"Read me some of it."

"First, let me take that mask off." She reached out and slipped it off. She winced at the sight but didn't feel the urge to run away. She saw him staring at her and asked, "what do you see?"

She was silhouetted by the flickering light of the fire. The shape of her wasn't prefect but he could recognise her head from the rest of her body. Her dress blurred the shape of her body as it spread out around her. He reached out to see if he could touch her but he didn't have the vision to discern such a short distance and missed her body so let his hand drop. She reached out and squeezed his hand, but he pulled it away, frustrated with his disability.

"Read to me." He said stiffly.

"Maybe I should find another book." She suggested.

"What other things could we have a try at?"
She opened to a page at random and began reading, "I soon perceived he had a mind to stick it in: first with his two fingers he opened the lips of my cunt, and thrust at me.."

He found himself putting his hand up under Nastasia's skirts as he lay with his eyes half shut, listening to her read and then describing the print she came to. Every so often Nastasia hesitated as she enjoyed Viktor's stroking. He recreated the scene she was describing with his fingers, pressing a finger inside only a short distance, teasing her.

She gave up reading and just lay back even though he said, "keep going."
She shook her head as she shifted her position and looked up into his face hoping for a kiss. She moaned with contentment at what he was doing and squirmed. If he had lain on top of her and pressed his penis against her she wouldn't have said no.

This was how Tamara found them.

They had heard the door but they were in their own little world and ignored it, they were both dressed. They looked as surprised as Tamara when she entered and called out, "Viktor?"

Viktor rolled over, removing his hand from under Nastasia's skirt as she hastily sat up. He asked in shock, "Tamara?! What are you doing here?"

"I had to see you considering… What is going on here? Where is your mask?"

"Nothing that you need to know about."

"What is Nastasia Balakina doing here?!" Tamara exclaimed as she saw Nastasia. She added with a hiss, "whore!"

"Tamara, this is none of your business." Viktor carefully stood.

"Does mother know what is happening here?"

"She does not need to know. It's my life and I can do what I want. I am asserting my independence. Just as you always wanted and Nastasia is no whore."

"She's only after one thing, just like her mother."

"You don't know her like I do." He protested, "she makes me feel alive. She doesn't care that I am blind."

"That's what she's been taught to do by her mother." Tamara attempted to reason with her brother.

"You are wrong!" Viktor shouted, "she's not like that! Go away!"
Nastasia stood under Tamara's glare and touched Viktor's arm, "perhaps I should go."
He turned, "no, stay, my sister will be the one to leave." He gripped her arm tight making her suck in her breath with pain.

"Not until she does." Tamara pointed at the other woman. Viktor's dog growled and then barked in reaction to the tension in the air.

Downstairs the Countess returned from seeing a friend and heard the barking. Fearing something had happened to Viktor she hurried to his rooms and saw her daughter first, "Tamara?!"

Tamara spun round and Viktor's head turned at his mother's voice. Nastasia pulled her arm out of Viktor's hand, grabbed her book and fled to his bedroom where she watched through the door. She prayed that the Countess hadn't seen her. She knew the woman had very little opinion of her and her mother.

Daria looked between her two children and then turned on her daughter, "what are you doing here? I thought I told you were not allowed to see Viktor. What were you arguing about?"

"Mother." Tamara exclaimed.

"You'll cause him to have a fit." Daria reprimanded, one eye on her angry son, his hands clenched as fists and looking red faced.

Tamara rolled her eyes in exasperation and said, "can you not see her?"

"See who?" Daria looked over her daughter's shoulder and only saw Viktor.

Tamara turned and looked shocked, "she was here."

"I think we need to take this discussion downstairs." Daria stepped out of the way and Tamara submitted and left the room.

Viktor called out, "what about me?"

"I'll talk to you later."

He stared at the door as it shut. He felt his fingers were itching to throw something. His mother had completely dismissed him. He found the back of the settle and pushed it over with a shout of anger. It crash to the floor.

Nastasia slowly opened the bedroom door, not sure what she was going to find on the other side. Seeing the pushed over settle she said, "I should go. Your mother doesn't like me."

"You don't have to go. I want you here and she can't stop it." He moved towards where he heard her voice. He found

an arm and pulled her towards him. He growled, "I want
you now."

"But your mother?" She hesitated. She was aroused but
the sight of the Countess had tempered it.

"Let her see." He held her close and she could feel his
desire in both his groin and his chest.

He pushed her towards his bed with a strength she
didn't realise he had. She tried to fight as she didn't like the
expression on Viktor's face. There was lust and anger
visibly on it, twisting his features. He held her arms in
place above her head. With the other he undid his breeches
and then pushed up her skirts. On his second attempt he
found the dark warm wetness of her sex that he craved. He
wanted his mother to walk in. He wanted her to see he was
a hot-blooded male; that he could do as he pleased now.
She needed him to be the heir so he would show her he was
capable of it!

She didn't want to be but she found herself
responding and tried to rise up but he pressed against her to
hard. Her eyes were wide from the fear and pleasure she
was feeling. Had she turned him into a monster?

He thrust into her again and again until with a loud
groan he came. He stepped back, panting.

She shuffled across the bed and sat up once she felt
far enough away from him. He looked up but couldn't
discern her body from the rest of the dimly lit bedroom. He
waved a hand at her, "you can go now."
She slipped off the bed, grabbed her fallen shoe that lay at
Viktor's feet and ran from the room. She surprised the
servants in their dining room, "Koplev get me a carriage."

The servants looked at each other and at Koplev. It
seemed their mistress had found the young master's
mistress. That had happened quicker than they thought.
One of the footmen smiled and held out a hand, "hand it all
over."

The others groaned, "later."

In the Countess' sitting room Tamara stood before her seated mother feeling like a little girl again.

Daria remained silent for effect. She wanted her daughter to be scared. She wanted to remind her daughter that she still could govern her even though she was a grown woman with a family of her own. Finally, she spoke, "I told you, you weren't allowed to see Viktor. I can't trust him with you and now I don't know whether I can trust you at all."

"He's my brother and I care for him." Tamara protested, "and had to see him since he's kept alone in his rooms. You are wrong to leave him there on his own."
Daria stood up, "how dare you speak to me like that? I am your mother and know best."

"Ha! Then do you know he has been having a visitor?"

Tamara watched her mother frown and then ask, "what visitor?"

"Nastasia Balakina." She smirked, glad she had got one over her own mother.

"Bitch." Daira spat in disgust. In a calmer voice that was stiff with reluctance she added, "thank you for that information. You are welcome here again Tamara." If Tamara was allow to visit again then Viktor would have no need for a whore. She gave her daughter a tight smile, "thank you. You may go now."

She took a deep breath as her daughter left. She realised she had been neglectful of her son. She still saw him as her little boy and clearly he had grown into a man with the needs of a man. At least in a few months he would be married. For now she would have to keep him away from Nastasia Balakina's manipulative influence.

She sat down at her writing desk to inform her husband to expect their son at their estate and sent it on its way. Then she went to speak with her son.

CHAPTER 11

Viktor was still angry with his mother for sending him to the family estate where the Count was busy watching over preparations for sowing the seed and recovering from the winter storms as well as ensuring the new supplies for their Empress' building projects. She claimed he needed to learn about running the estate from his father. He had angrily objected till she had decreed he was having one of his fits and ordered Koplev to hold him down till he calmed down.

His father was dressed as a country gentleman in knee length boots over loose trousers and a fine woollen loose shirt with an embroidered bottom edge. He stood on the steps as the carriage drew up. He chuckled to himself. His wife had been a bit over dramatic over their son having a mistress, barely even a mistress. On the positive side it would be good to have some time with his son, man to man.

Borya jumped out of the carriage first as Tverdislav came down the steps, "welcome Viktor."

"Hmpfh."

"Come, I know your mother has overreacted, but it will be good to have some time together." He remarked as his son carefully stepped from the carriage, "it will do you some good to be away from your mother and learn more about how to run the estate. Now, you must be tired, so we'll have a quiet evening and then tomorrow we'll head out."

With relief Viktor pulled the mask off and felt the cool air on his warm skin. He knew his father would punish any serf who might react poorly to his appearance.

The following day the Count led his son round the

estate on horseback, holding Viktor's horse with a leading rein. Viktor felt the power trembling in the horse and wished he could gallop off on it. He glowered at his father's back without realising he was making the bowing serfs wary of him. The children tried not to stare at their lord's disfigurement and received hissed threats from their parents for staring.

The afternoon was spent more pleasantly by the river fishing for their dinner. Borya ran up and down the riverbank following various smells that interested him but always returned to his master. Fishing was something he could do once the gamekeeper had baited the hook. He could feel the fish struggling on the end of the line through the vibrations that ran up the rod, "I've got one."

"Let's get it in."

Viktor stepped back and pulled the fish in with a grin, "how big is it?"

"A tiddler." His father teased.

"What?! It feels bigger than that."

"I'm teasing." Tverdislav laughed, "it's a good size, now we need a few more." He nodded at the gamekeeper who put the caught fish in a bucket before putting fresh bait on Viktor's line. As the servant stepped back Tverdislav returned to the earlier conversation and asked, "so how was it?"

"Good, until Tamara appeared and told mother."

"At least you can see Tamara again."

"Hmm."

"Think it's my turn with a fish." The Count turned his attention to the vibrating fishing rod.

"I'm not giving her up." Viktor blurted out, surprising his father who then lost his fish.

Tverdislav turned and stared at his son. Wary of the answer, he asked, "what do you want to do?"

"I want her, I need her."

"We can't back out of the betrothal, and she isn't wife material."

"How do you know? You haven't spoken to her?" He turned to face his father, "she…. She…." He couldn't find the words to explain what Nastasia meant to him. He bit his bottom lip as he tried to make sense of what he thought about Nastasia Balakina. He was intoxicated by her. Just catching her scent as she came close made him want her. It wasn't just the sex either. With her around he was left feeling good about himself, that his injuries paled into insignificance. She saw him, not the scars.

"Viktor." Tverdislav put a hand on his son's arm, "she's born outside of marriage to a man's mistress. She is not a good prospect for a wife. Look… Enjoy her, use her but know you can not marry her. You are to marry Katerina Livovna. She comes from a good family and she comes with a good dowry which we need as our Empress doesn't pay all her bills. She looks after her father's household and so will be able to run your household when I am gone."

"But I don't feel anything for her."

"You will with time. I didn't always love your mother." Tverdislav said and wondered when he had fallen out of love with his wife. He sighed.

"Was mother always the way she is now?" Viktor asked as he noted the tension in his father's sigh.

"No." Tverdislav looked out on the river as he tried to remember his wife as the young girl. He smiled as he remembered the youthful sexual discoveries they had, just as Viktor was discovering now. She began to change when Viktor had been injured. After a few years with several miscarriages and no other sons born they had gone their separate ways. She had concentrated all her emotions on Viktor and now Viktor was resisting and the family was becoming estranged again. He looked at Viktor and wondered what life would have been like if it wasn't for the

bear. What could his son have become? He'd have joined
one of the regiments and made a fine officer "Viktor?"

"Mmm…."

"Just keep going but be careful." He couldn't believe that
he was actually encouraging his son to rebel against his
mother but he knew he couldn't stop his son and in honesty
he didn't want to. He hoped that Daria would eventually
see the man rather than the boy she wanted him to remain.
A small smile played on his lips.

CHAPTER 12

Nastasia watched as the Medvedev's carriage drew up. She had missed Viktor as well as the fact Katerina would still not see her. When she had heard nothing from him she had made enquiries from a sneering manservant that Viktor had been sent to the family's country estate in disgrace because of her. He had laughed at her and she realised how low she had fallen, all because of her mother; because of his mother. She wasn't sure who to blame more. If she was more vindictive, she would have taken revenge on Viktor's mother for separating them.

If she could just see Viktor maybe he would set up a home of her own and then she would earn some respect back. Then he could come to her and she wouldn't have to sneak around.

She resisted the urge to see if the servants would let her in. She would wait to see if Viktor would send for her. She turned and walked away and hoped her mother wouldn't mock her for moping around like a needy puppy again.

Inside Viktor's shoulders sagged as he was taken back to his suite of rooms. Although he had been angry at being sent to the estate by the third day he had enjoyed it. He had enjoyed being in his father's company. They had ridden out most days, fished and talked. He even joined his father and his friends for dinner after a day of hunting and the men had followed the Count's lead and treated him as a man even though there were glances at the scarring. He'd even been involved in a locally organised sword fighting competition. He worked off all his excess energy and frustrations. If he had concentrated more he probably would have won but his thoughts were all over the place.

On the estate they all knew of what had happened and no one stared apart from children. He wondered if he could just live on the estate with Nastasia. His soon to be wife could live in St Petersburg and follow the court round if she wanted to. On the estate he could be his own person, in the city he was his mother's doll; something to pick up and abandon whenever she wanted and if anyone else showed too much interest in him that was when she would fight and demand him back. He thought of Tamara and wondered if he could turn her opinion round to support him again. He couldn't have her on their mother's side as well. Nastasia wasn't a whore.

Now he was back under his mother's overprotective eye, but his father had promised to speak to her. He wondered whether he should send for Nastasia just to annoy his mother and then wished he had been able to let Nastasia know where he had gone. He called out, "Koplev?"

"Sir?"

"Sort out a gift for Nastasia and send it to her with an invite for two days' time to come and visit." Hopefully his mother would have forgotten about him again by then.

"Yes sir." Koplev rolled his eyes, so much for the Countess thinking that time away from St Petersburg would cool his young master's desires.

Downstairs the Countess couldn't believe what she was hearing and protested, "no. She is not welcome here. She's just like her mother and see how that affected Liv Antonovich."

"He is a man and not a little boy and has been for the last fifteen years. At least she is clean and not seeing others. He has agreed to end it when he marries Katerina Livovna and there is nothing wrong with Liv Antonovich."

"Hmpfh."

"Can I remind you that this is my family and home as

well."

Her eyes widened. She rarely saw her husband angry. Normally he left everything to her to deal with for the sake of peace. Once they might have loved each other but Viktor's injuries had put a strain on their marriage and still did. Their opinions on how Viktor should live always conflicted, like now. Regretfully she submitted, "fine, as long as it does end."

"It will." He answered firmly.

Nastasia eagerly and nervously appeared at the invited time and Koplev led her upstairs. He left her by the door, not even bothering to announce her attendance making her wonder what was going on with the servant. He was normally more cordial. She opened the door to Viktor's sitting room, "Viktor?"

She saw him on a window seat bathed in the warm light of a spring day. His hands stroked Borya as his back rested against the side wall of the window alcove. He turned with a smile that softened the edges of his scars, "Nastasia? Come and join me by the window."

Borya greeted her with a sniff and lick of her hands as she came and joined him by the window. The light made his pale blonde hair appear like white gold and he looked surprisingly well.

He reached out and found her knee, "I'm sorry that I couldn't tell you where I was going; it all happened so fast. Did you get the gift?"

"Your servant has a good eye. You look well."

"I feel well, and you?"

She shied away from answered, "what did you do?"

"I spent time with my father." Viktor smiled before going on to tell her everything. She sat listening politely and when she couldn't distract him any longer she lied about what she had been up to.

They spent most of the afternoon talking. It was as if two weeks apart had cooled the sexual flames between them and though they both felt the desire they could control it. Today was a day to get to know each other. They spoke of childhoods, of books and of family. By the end Nastasia felt that she had a friend for life and not just a lover. She gave him a kiss filled with promise before she left. His hold lingered on her arm full of wistfulness before reluctantly letting her go. Tomorrow was another day.

Katerina heard that Viktor had returned from the family estate and knew that she needed to get to him before Nastasia got her claws back in him. She needed to remind him that they were to be married and if he respected her he would stay away from her half-sister.

She was greeted by the Countess who was looking forward to having her as a daughter-in-law and as another person who could watch over and protect her son. She thought Katerina would be meek enough that she could control her and remain in charge of her son's care.

After having made polite conversation with the Countess she was allowed upstairs. She heard voices on the other side of the door and paused with her hand on the handle. She heard a moan and it wasn't one of pain. With a shaking hand she quietly opened the door out of fear and curiosity. All she could see was the back of Nastasia's head with her hair spilling over the back of the settle. She watched as Nastasia arched her neck and her mouth opened in ecstasy.

A sob of angst escaped Katerina's mouth. She put a hand to her mouth to try and stifle another one, but it was too late.

Nastasia sat up and put a hand on Viktor's head to stop him. From where he knelt between her thighs he leant back, "what is it?"

"I thought I heard something."

"It was probably Borya."

"It wasn't him." She turned her head and saw the door was open, "we are being spied on." She hastily adjusted her skirts, hiding Viktor in them.

He fought his way out of the multiple layers and sought out his mask before standing revealing his undone waistcoat. He demanded, "who is there? Reveal yourself."

"How could you Nastasia?!" Katerina exclaimed as she showed herself.

"I could say the same to you." Nastasia retorted as she stood.

"Katerina?" Viktor was surprised, he hadn't been expecting a visit from his betrothed.

"This is meant to be a time for us to get to know each other but instead I find you here with a whore who..." Katerina couldn't even think of her as a sister at that moment.

"I was not expecting a visit from you."

"Should I have warned you so you could have hidden her rather than have her rubbed in my face." She spat in anger. She blocked Nastasia out but was convinced she was grinning, enjoying her discomfort.

"I can do what I want. You do not rule me."

"I am your betrothed and I came to see you." Her voice pleaded.

"And you still are. And until we are married I can do as I please."

"But why her?" She protested.

"Viktor?" Nastasia murmured. She put a hand on his arm. He leant towards her as she added, "perhaps you should do something with her. If you want to continue seeing me you will need to placate Katerina."

Katerina watched with growing distress as Viktor leant into Nastasia. She saw how comfortable they were around each other and wanted that. Hurt was turning to jealousy. Nastasia had grabbed the bull and won while she had meekly stood by as the dutiful daughter. Was that all she would be? A dutiful obedient daughter then dutiful nursemaid wife? Her mother-in-law had made it clear what her role would be, nurse to Viktor and carrier of the future heir to the Medvedev name. Now she wasn't so sure. The good thing was she would be safe and secure as a wife and Nastasia would be a mistress who could be dropped by Viktor whenever he chose.

"I..." Viktor stumbled over his words.

"I mean once you are also married." Nastasia interrupted quietly before he could object, "and I don't think a gift will be enough."

He nodded when he realised what she meant. He turned to face the direction he had last heard Katerina, "what can I do to make you happy?"

"Stop seeing that whore on your arm." Katerina demanded.

"That," He said sternly, "I will not do."

Katrina thought Nastasia looked triumphant and realised she had demanded too much straight away. She realised she would have to build up to it if she was to win against the witch Nastasia. She changed tact, "perhaps we could go for a walk or carriage ride?"

"That sounds like a nice idea." He answered with relief and a smile.

She didn't.

Viktor had now lost interest "I think you should both go now."

"What? Why? What have I done? She was the one who intruded on us." Nastasia protested now. More than ever she now needed to convince Viktor to get her a little apartment they could use for the sake of privacy.

"I'm no longer in the mood for your company."

It was Katerina's turn to look triumphant.

Nastasia scowled at her half sister. She turned to Viktor and put on a smile as she asked with forced brightness, "when will I see you again?"

"I'll send a message." He answered stiffly, "Katerina, I'll collect you at eleven."

"Thank you." Katerina responded tensely while glaring at Nastasia.

The following day Katerina didn't care that most of the ride to the tree edged Summer Garden, which included the little used Summer Palace of Peter the Great, was done in silence. The trees were starting to unfurl their leaves. Soon the gardens on the island would be hidden from the view of from anyone sailing by one of the three rivers and the canal that created the land into an island. She had got Viktor away from Nastasia and now it was time to remind him that he was soon to be married to her and that he would need to give Nastasia up.

As they walked the statue lined pathways and pass the fountains, she tucked her hands into his elbow while Borya walked by Viktor's side. Other courtiers with permission to use the Summer Garden to stroll glanced curiously across and then talked amongst themselves. Katerina leant against Viktor as she remarked, "this is what it's supposed to be like."

"I don't want to hear about it. We are doing this because you wanted to."

Her eyes cast downwards and she straightened. She didn't like this new Viktor. She remarked carefully, "she has changed you."

"She has made me a man." He stood taller, feeling full of pride, "which will mean I will be a better husband."

She blushed, getting the meaning behind his words. She supposed she should be thankful but she had hoped they would learn together.

"Are you looking forward to our marriage?" He asked with stiff politeness, trying to hide the face he wanted to be anywhere else but in the gardens. He would have preferred Nastasia on his arm.

"Yes and no." She answered with relief that he was trying to bridge the space that had formed between them. She was scared of leaving her father on his own and that he might move his long time mistress in. Then there was moving in with the Medvedevs and whether the Countess would allow her to be a wife and carer to Viktor without interfering. And there was the most important duty of a wife, would she be able to give him the requisite heir?

"Oh? Don't be scared. I know my family like you." He tried to reassure her.

"Thank you."

CHAPTER 13

As the wedding drew closer he knew he needed to wean himself off Nastasia. He had promised his father it would end and didn't want to let him down. The problem was he was finding it hard. He looked forward to hearing her footsteps and her voice. He loved the smell of her and to feel her warm skin in his hands and hearing her enjoy herself. He didn't want to give her up.

Though their love making had relaxed it had recently developed an urgency again. They had become wary to every noise and feared being found by either his mother, sister and now also Katerina. But Nastasia was becoming demanding. She kept suggesting he sort out an apartment for her that he could then visit but remembering the promise to his father he didn't react to her obvious suggestions. He was also trying to workout his feelings towards her. Could he love her? How could he knowing he was to marry Katerina? What did she feel for him? Could they somehow keep it going without any emotional entanglement?

Instead he did the cowardly thing and asked Tamara if he could stay with her for a while. He was honest with her and if it meant he could end his developing habit of Nastasia then she was very willing to let him stay with her family. He wanted the freedom Tamara's home gave him which his mother was restricting.

It felt like she was suffocating him again as well as the snide remarks she was making about Nastasia. He tried not to get angry at his mother when she did, but he had once and there had been a triumphant tone in her voice as she decreed he was having one of his fits which was why she knew best. He wanted to keep his newfound independence. He didn't want to remain a prisoner with his mother as goaler and then his wife. He couldn't work out what Katerina wanted. Probably because he had been willingly preoccupied with Nastasia.

As Borya and Tamara led him into her home his nephews were there to greet him having persuaded their tutor to let them out of their lessons. They ran through the rooms to the front door and skidded to a stop. Lev exclaimed, "mama said you were coming." He bent and gave Borya a stroke as the dog wagged its tail.

"Shouldn't you be learning?" Viktor remarked with a smile.

"Well..." Ilya pulled a face, "it's always nice to see you."

"I'm glad to hear that, and as a reward for saying such nice things I think there are some soldiers to add to your collection."

"Did you have any?" Lev asked out of curiosity as he took his uncle's hand and led him up to Tamara's sitting room.

"I can't remember."
Ilya remarked, "how could he play with them if he couldn't see them?"
Lev stuck his tongue out at his brother.

"Boys." Tamara said sternly.

"Sorry mama, sorry uncle."

"That's all right. Go and find Koplev." Viktor replied. Ilya ran out of the room. Lev hesitated a moment before letting go of his uncle's hand and hurrying after his twin brother.

"And where is Anna?"

"At a dance lesson." Tamara replied as she guided her brother on to a settle before ringing for a maid.

"They are good children. Let's hope any I have will be like them."

"I'm sure they will. Are you ready for the wedding?"

"As much as I can be."

"We are out at the theatre in a few nights time, will you
be all right on your own?"

"Of course."

"The children shouldn't bother you."

"I wouldn't mind if they did." He smiled. He enjoyed
being around his nephews when they were allowed away
from the watchful eyes of their tutor and nursemaid.

Over the next two days he kept Tamara company in
her sitting room while she dealt with her daily duties as
mistress of the house. Anna would come and read to them
and get wrongly pronounced words corrected by both her
mother and uncle. In the evening Ilya and Lev came to
show their parents what they had learnt that day before
going back to the nursery for their dinner.

On the evening of Tamara and Gravil going to the
theatre the children were seen early. Tamara gave her
brother a kiss before they went out, "take care of yourself."

"Enjoy yourselves."

"Are you sure you will be all right?"

"Koplev will look after me." He reassured her.

With his sister and brother-in-law gone he had
dinner and went to bed with Koplev's help. He lay in bed
trying not to think of Nastasia. It had only been two days
but already he was yearning for her. He tried to distract
himself by thinking of his coming marriage then his mind
would start to see if he could have both of them but he
knew his allowance wasn't enough for an apartment plus
the servants and clothes Nastasia would need. In fact he
had no idea what his allowance was or who watched over
it.

He didn't know when he fell asleep but he woke as
the atmosphere felt different. He heard Borya barking and
realised that was why he had woken up. The air around him
felt hot and seemed to crackle. He raised himself on to his

elbows and called out, "Koplev?! Tamara?!"
The sound of crackling became louder and he was sure he could smell smoke. He heard cracking above his head and looked up. A piece of burning wood fell from the ceiling. Feeling the heat on his right arm he flinched away in alarm. Even if he didn't know what was going on he knew what fire felt like. He began to panic as he felt his bedding begin to burn. The building was burning around him and he didn't know if he was going to be remembered as everyone else fled.

He slipped from his bed to get away from his burning bedding, falling to the floor, as he was tangled in the sheets. He heard the hungry flames consuming his bed and spreading. As he got to his feet he felt the floorboards heating up through the soles of his bare feet. With hands outstretched he began to inch round the bed in the hope of finding a wall and then the door. He had to retreat when he felt the heat of flames in front of him.

He sidestepped away from the bed and found Borya who was scratching at the door, "good boy."
He opened the door and staggered through and fell to his knees, coughing from the smoke. There was a whoosh as the fire started consuming the fresh oxygen. On hands and knees he crawled away. Borya was already at the next door. Viktor coughed and called out, "help!"
He didn't know if Tamara had returned home or whether anyone had realised the house was on fire. He carefully stood and shouted in the hope of waking the household up, "fire! Fire!" With a whimper he ended, "please wake up."

He turned on the spot but only because he had never felt so disorientated in his life, even more so then when he had been at the palace. There was the powerful cough inducing smell of smoke and the sounds of crackling flames plus a barking and scrabbling Borya. It was all crowding his senses so it was hard to concentrate on Borya.

He felt the heat at his back and knew he was facing the right way.

Outside Tamara and Gravil's carriage pulled up with the coachman barely controlling a pair of horses that were reacting to the danger they could sense. Stepping from their carriage they stared up in growing horror at the red and orange glow on the top floors of the building where their large apartment was. Smoke was coming through the windows and finding gaps in the roof. There was a crash as a part of the roof collapsed, waking the couple up. They broke into a run as thoughts of their children came to the top of their minds. Gravil burst into the building shouting, "fire! Get up!"

He took the stairs two at a time and crashed through their front door, arm up to protect against the heat. His damp sleeve steamed from the heat. Tamara was behind him and he shouted, "stay back."
He could image her skirts catching alight. There was a wail from Anna's room as she woke to find her room filled with smoke. Tamara threw the door open and grabbed hold of her daughter and shielded her as they hurried back down the stairs. Behind her the twins' nursemaid and Gravil followed with the twins. As they reached the outdoors a few servants had appeared as well as the rest of the building's residents.

They watched the fire spread to the next building as the interior burst into flames from the heat. There were enough people now to start a bucket chain to try and combat the spreading of the flames. A few were praying for rain. More of the roof collapsed and flames shot upwards. Tamara started to work out who she had of her household. She spotted Koplev looking after two maids. She span round then and shouted, "Viktor?! Viktor?!"
She saw Koplev look up and she realised then that her

104

brother wasn't with them. She turned to her husband, "Viktor is still in there."

With a sigh he reluctantly said, "I'll go."

"No." She responded fiercely, "he's my responsibility. Keep hold of the children." She pushed her crying daughter at Gravil and ran back in before he could stop her. Gravil turned to the gathered servants and shouted, "Koplev, get in there. My wife is doing your job."

Inside, Viktor, arms out in front of him, shied backwards as burning wood fell near by. Borya still barked and he shuffled forward again, stubbing a foot on a piece of furniture. He shuffled sideways and took cautious steps forward. He sighed with some relief as he found a door. He opened it and Borya ran out, nearly tripping Tamara up.

She shouted in surprise and nearly fell backwards. Righting herself she tore her skirt off as it was beginning to burn. She called out with a cough, "Viktor?!"

She spotted him coming out of a door and grabbed his arm. He twisted his arm and locked his hand on the arm, "Tamara?"

"It's me. I'll get you out."

He grabbed her arm with his free hand as she led him towards the stairs.

Her foot went through the floor. She cried out and let go of Viktor. He waved his arms before him in fear, "Tamara?!"

"Get Gravil Viktor, please. Go get help." She could feel heat on the sole of her foot, her shoe having fallen to the floor below. She cried out as the hole grew bigger and she began to fall through it.

He followed her voice to the floor and felt her reach for his hand. She said with fear, "pull me up."

He grabbed hold of her arm and tried to pull her up. He struggled but managed to pull her up by several inches. She began to slip out of his sweaty hands and then she wasn't there. It happened too fast for her to make a sound as she fell to the floor below, burning timbers raining down on her. Viktor cried out.

Koplev ran up the stairs and through the door. He grabbed Viktor's leg and dragged him away from the hole in the floor. Viktor fought back, "no! No! Tamara!"

"Viktor!" Gravil shouted angrily and the man froze. Koplev pulled Viktor towards him and tore off a strip of linen from his night shirt and tied it round the young man's head to hide the childhood wounds. Viktor made to pull it off. Now was not the time to be worrying about embarrassing his mother. His hand was slapped away. He tried to break away from Koplev's strong grip, "Tamara is still in there. She might be alive."

"You aren't going anywhere." Koplev hissed, "your life is more important than hers."

Viktor turned to face his servant, "how dare you?!" With his free hand he thumped Koplev, hoping to hit his face. Koplev staggered backwards, bumping into Gravil.

Gravil turned and saw Viktor stagger back towards the building. He grabbed his brother-in-law, "no you don't. I don't want your she-devil of a mother accusing me of letting you die as well. She'll curse me." He threw Viktor to the ground to keep him from doing anything stupid.

The three men's heads turned as they heard a cry. Tamara called out again, "help."

Gravil ran through the open door and through the building. To have heard her meant she was near by.

Minutes later Gravil appeared, clothes smoking and carrying his wife in his arms.

"The horses are out of control sir." The coachman was fighting the rearing horses while inside the carriage Anna and the twins cried out in fear and for their mother. Viktor huddled in a corner of the carriage, gulping in lungfuls of air.

"I thought you were supposed to be good with horses."
Gravil snapped at the driver.
Koplev came to help the coachman as Gravil got into the
carriage with the help of his manservant.

Reaching the Medevdevs' house the children were
soon back in beds, snuffling, under the close eye of their
nurse. Gravil was thankful they were unharmed unlike his
wife. She lay so still, her arms and face covered with red
burns that he didn't know if she was alive until a moan
would shudder through her body. The Countess watched
over her daughter with Gravil as the doctor frowned. When
he looked up Gravil demanded, "well?"
"If she survives the night then there is hope. Where is the
other patient?"
"You are staying here." Gravil ordered.
The Countess put a hand on his arm and softly said, "stay
with her in case she wakes." To the family's doctor she
added, "this way."
Gravil sank into a chair to watch his wife and silently pray
that she would survive. He didn't know what he would do
if she died. This was Viktor's fault. If he had been able to
get out himself she wouldn't have had to go in for him. He
reasoned in his grief, 'if she died her brother would feel his
rage.'

Viktor was given a sleeping draught and Tverdislav
looked down at his sleeping son and saw the little boy that
they had fretted over. He was glad his son wasn't more
seriously hurt as Viktor's face pinched up with pain. Viktor
lay on his side with blackened tipped hair where it had
singed in the heat. His burnt right arm was now bandaged
after a salve had been put on it.
He turned as his wife returned from checking their

daughter, "how is she?"

"She hasn't woken. What have we done to anger God?" He shrugged, his faith in God was not the strongest since Viktor lost his sight.

"We must pray for forgiveness." She answered her own question and wondered if she should have the priest sent for.

A howl of grief and rage echoed through the house. The children sat up in their beds and looked at each other with wide eyed fear. Tverdislav and Daria sat up in the chairs they were in. Daria was on her feet first and through the bedroom door as her husband rubbed sleep from his eyes. Before he could stand she reappeared, all colour drained from her face. He found himself whispering, "Daria?"

"She's dead." The Countess whispered as an anguished sob came from Gravil who knelt at the side of the bed.

Tverdislav was startled by the man's reaction. As for himself he felt drained of emotion. His daughter was dead and he wasn't sure how to react. Yes, he was upset about it but how were they going to tell Viktor? They had been so close. As tears ran down her face Daria was worrying about the same thing, "how do we tell Viktor?"
She paused and when she got no answer from her husband she decided, "we'll tell him after the funeral."

"He'll know something is happening." He said, breaking his silence.

"Not in his rooms he won't." She answered.
He scowled at her and stood. He had had enough. He wanted to mourn in peace and on his own.

Daria thought about stopping him from going but dropped her hand before she could. Now wasn't the time to try and get him back on her side over Viktor, over their shrinking family. Two deaths within a year of each other was two too many.

She needed to blame someone as sorrow turned to anger. This was Nastasia Balakina's fault. If she hadn't weaseled her way into Viktor's life he wouldn't have gone to Tamara's for whatever reason he never told her and Tamara would never have had to go back into find him. He wasn't anyone else's but hers. He needed to survive for the family name, to prove she could have children that were strong and healthy. That was the only reason she had let him have fencing lessons to show that he was fit and well but no one saw it. It was to reassure herself.

CHAPTER 14

There was an all-night vigil before the funeral with prayers led by the family's priest and then psalms read from the Book of Psalms. The room was filled with friends and family. The only one missing was Viktor who sat and slept, oblivious, confined to his suite of rooms and allowed no visitors, raging over it. His furniture was turned over or broken. Not even Alla dared enter. He didn't even know Nastasia had sent him a message. His mother intercepted it, screwed it up and thrown it in the fire to get back her control of him.

He was sat, still, as if he was a statue and not a person, at his table in the window, a hand resting on the foot of a wine glass when Katerina entered with a knock. She opened the door and peered round, "Viktor Tverdislavich?"
He cocked his head and asked with surprise, "Katerina?"
"It is. How are you Viktor? How is your arm?" She asked with concern. She approached and sat beside him. She reached out and touched his hand and watched him flinch away from her touch before relaxing and taking her hand in his.
"Sore. Do you know anything about Tamara? No one is telling me anything." His hand squeezed hers so tight she had to bite her lip not to cry out. She released her held breath as the grip relaxed. She had heard what had happened to Tamara but knew it wasn't her place to tell, "err… no."
"Oh…" He replied with disappointment. "One moment I expect her to come through the door, the next I fear she is dead." He gripped the stem of the glass so tight it looked like it would break as he remembered her slipping from her

hands and her cry as she fell through the floor.

She reached out and took his hand again, "perhaps we should pray."
He pulled his hand away, he didn't want to pray to a God that tortured him.

"He sends us tests for a reason." She softly suggested, sensing his reluctance. When he didn't respond except to take hold of the empty glass again she made to leave. She was halfway to the door when there were angry footsteps outside it and the door flew open.

Gravil stormed in, tear trails glistening on his cheeks and red rimmed eyes. He didn't even notice Katerina who quickly moved out of his way. His eyes were set on Viktor who was now standing. Borya growled. Viktor cautiously asked, "Gravil?"

"Don't Gravil me." The elder man snapped, "if it hadn't been for you Tamara would still be alive. You should have died a long time ago. You feed off others."

Viktor looked shocked. One hand gripped the table to hold himself up, "Tamara..."
Gravil, in two large steps, reached the blind man and grabbed hold of Viktor, "don't say that name! You don't deserve to even mouth it! I loved her even if she didn't love me. It's because of you that she no longer lives."

"No longer lives…?" Viktor repeated. He didn't try to fight the hold Gravil had on him.

"Yes. Soon she will be before God but you should be the one up there, not her."

"I..." Viktor didn't know what to say.

"Don't speak." Gravil ordered. He lifted Viktor up and threw him across the room.
Viktor crashed against his chair by the fireplace. Gravil stalked out of the room as Borya barked and Viktor curled up where he lay.

With Gravil gone, Katerina ran across the room to

Viktor. She knelt down beside him and reached out, "Viktor?"

He moaned as tears ran down his face, "she's gone." Katerina put her arms round him and gently rocked him. Softly she said, "I'm not going anywhere."

"She's dead." He said mournfully.

"Her soul will be watching over you for a few days yet." She tried to reassure him.

"They didn't tell me." He moaned, "she has been buried and I wasn't even there. Mother has kept me away again."

"She only wants to protect you."

"I don't need to be protected." He protested though the tears renewed themselves and he clutched at the fabric of her skirt with a tight fist. She looked down at him and wished she could help him. Then she had an idea to cleave him to her, "maybe this is God punishing you?"

"For what?" He looked up with fear.

She bit her lip before saying, "for sleeping with Nastasia." He sat up, his lips pressed firmly together, "I think you should go."

She froze, it hadn't worked.

"Go!" He snapped and pushed her away, "do not speak of Nastasia like that."

She shuffled backwards and fled as he slowly stood. She didn't like his anger, she felt afraid of it and she felt sure it came from being with Nastasia. She paused at the door and watched him grab the side table and turn it over as he wordlessly raged.

He didn't want it to be a warning from God. He didn't want to believe that Tamara was gone and he was the last to know. He didn't want to lose Nastasia from his life. He didn't want to be protected by anyone.

His parents found him huddled in a corner with his mask lying at his feet and most of the furniture lying on its side again. He was dry eyed when he looked up at his parents' footsteps, "why did God have to take her? She never did any wrong."

The Countess knelt by her son and held him close. He leant against her as she asked, "how did you find out?"

"Gravil blames me. Was it my fault?"

"You weren't to know that a fire would start." She tried to console him.

"Why didn't you tell me when it happened? It's not fair."

"We didn't want to lose you as well. I know how much you loved Tamara."

"I'm stronger than you think." He protested and tried to get away from her, but she held him tight.

She said with concern, "this crying and raging will not have done you much good. Let's get you to bed."

"No." He began to fight his mother's hold. He knew what would come next and he didn't want to be drugged, "no, no, no. I'm not a child who doesn't know what you are doing."

"We can't have you having another fit." She looked to her husband for support.

"Leave him to mourn." Tverdislav said.

Daria glared at him for not supporting her.

Tverdislav kept his eyes cast down for he felt if she caught his eye he would capitulate. He wanted to be on his son's side. He wanted him to be treated as a man.

"No. He will make himself ill." His wife protested.

"He is no longer a child remember." He said sternly.

She glared at him and then walked from the room. She wasn't going to win this time.

The Count righted his son's chair and with a father's love led his son to it, "I'm sorry. Your mother is a strong-willed woman."

"Sir?"

"Now," his father sat down himself and leant forward, "mourn your sister but don't make it hard for her to leave this world. Her spirit will be making sure everyone will be able to carry on without her. You must show it that you are strong.”

“I want to go to her grave.”

“In six days once she has ascended to the Lord's Presence. We don't want to give her an excuse to stay.” Viktor turned away from his father.

The Count sighed. He had no idea how to get through to his son. Just as he had told his wife they were going to have let Viktor find his own path to mourning.

CHAPTER 15

Nastasia sat in her room chewing on a well bitten nail hiding from her mother. With no plans to go out she wore a simple linen blouse with a lace and ribbon edged green sarafan. Her hair was one long plait down her back. All her thoughts were about Viktor, why hadn't he replied to her note? How injured was he? She wanted to tell him she was sorry about his sister but it was like he had disappeared. Had he forgotten about her that quickly? She just wanted to see him and check he was alive. Any burn scars couldn't be any worse than the scars of his face.

She missed him. He was like Katerina in the early days of their sisterhood, accepting of her and didn't care about what her mother was. She knew they made each other happy but a wedding would soon separate them. She wanted to talk to him, persuade him that they could stay together.

She was startled out of her thoughts by a knock at her bedroom door. The door crept open, and the maid peered round, wary of Nastasia's reaction, "miss?"

"Yes?"

"There is a gentleman here to see you."

"Did he give a name?" She frowned.

"No."

"Fine." Nastasia sighed, "I'm coming."

"He…. He… is rather ugly." The maid admitted. Nastasia's eyes widened. Could it be?

She hurried past the maid and into the sitting room. She recognised that hair, "Viktor?!"

He turned, "I had to see you. I had to get away. I snuck out via the kitchens." He laughed but it came across forced.

"Where's your mask?" She asked in shock. She stepped closer and then retreated as he reeked of vodka.

"Fuck the mask. Fuck my mother."

"Is Koplev here?" She looked towards the door hoping the manservant would come and take control. She had never seen Viktor like this reminding herself she barely knew him.

"I sent him home." He sneered, "I don't need a servant watching me. I bet he reports back to my bitch mother every move I make."

"I don't think so. Anna," she turned to the maid, "see if there is a man leaving by the name of Koplev downstairs."

"Are you sure?" She asked warily, not liking the visitor's behaviour.

"I'll be alright." Nastasia said softly so as not to escalate the situation, "just go."

The maid ran, slamming the front door making Nastasia wince and Viktor twitch.

"I'm not going back there." He exclaimed, "I'll stay here with you."

"You can't."

He staggered towards her. He wanted her so badly, a taste of the forbidden fruit, just to show his mother. He reached for her but missed. She stepped sideways and crossed her arms, "I think you should go home. I don't want to see you when you are like this."

"Like what? Like a man?" He sneered and tried to stand up straighter.

"You aren't touching me." She exclaimed.

"I own you."

She didn't like this nasty streak Viktor had revealed with too much drinking. She braced herself to defend herself. This was like one of those moments when a drunk stranger at a party tried to kiss her, "you don't own me."

He reached out for her again and she slapped his hand away.

He sneered, "you don't do that to me. I know you want me.

116

I want you."

"No. You are mourning your sister." She side stepped
him again as he crashed into her mother's side table. She
took a deep breath and slapped him hard. He shook his
head and put a hand to where it hurt. The tears began to fall
then, taking her by surprise.

Carefully she took his hand. He let her lead him to
the privacy of her room just in case her mother came home.
She knew the maid and cook would look after Koplev.

She pressed him down on to her bed and then
crouched down in front of him. She held his hands in her's.
Looking up into his stubbly tear-stained face she said
softly, "let it out and then be strong. From what you have
told me of your sister she wouldn't want to see you like
this. She was always trying to help you but now you must
help her. Her spirit won't want to leave if you don't show
her that you can survive without her. Your father cares
about you. I care about you." She held tight to his hands as
with a sterner tone she went on, "carry on like this and your
mother will carry on seeing you as a boy and not the man I
know you are."
He slowly blinked and brushed the tears and snot away
with the sleeve of his shirt, "you are right."
She stood up and then sat on her bed so her back was
against the headboard, "come here."
He turned round and crawled up the bed.

He lay his head on her lap. In the silence she
stroked his hair. He had run out of tears but every so often
his whole body shuddered with a silent sob. If he could see,
he would be staring blankly across the room.

He felt overwrought with emotion. He was angry at
his parents for the way they treated him. He was also angry
at Tamara for dying. Then there was himself. He felt sorry
for himself and wanted to wallow in self-pity. He feared
what Gravil would do for he would miss his nephews if he

couldn't see them. He was annoyed with Katerina for trying to manipulate him. And then there was Nastasia. He didn't want to lose her as well but knew he was going to have to, and he didn't know how she would react when he told her.

Finally his breathing slowed and there were no more sudden intakes and releases of breath. He had fall asleep and Nastasia sighed with relief. She slipped out from under him and covered him with one of her blankets.

He woke up to the scent of Nastasia on the pillow and buried his face in it. He breathed in deep. A hand sought for her but found an empty bed. He realised then that it wasn't his bed and his mouth felt dry. He sat up, "Nastasia?"
The door opened and there were footsteps he recognised, "Nastasia, where am I?"
"You came to me." She smiled softly.
"Oh…."
"Are you feeling better?"
"I…." Then he remembered he had been a mess in front of Nastasia, "I'm sorry."
"That's alright. I'm glad you felt you could." She sat down on the bed and squeezed his hand, "I wanted to come and see you. How burnt were you?"
"Just my arm…."
"Does it need any attention?"
He chose to misconstrue her innocent question and turned over the hand she held to stroke her palm. She looked down at his hand and then into his red rimmed eyes. Softly she asked, "are you sure?"
"Only if you are."
She leant in and cupped his head with one hand which he leant against as she kissed him. She came up for air and held his head in both hands. She studied his face, "I'm here for you and I see you for the man you are, for the man

Tamara thought you could be."

He nodded as tears beaded in the remains of his eyes. She kissed them away.

They lay down facing each other, faces so close they were breathing each other's air. Their hands rested on each other, and Viktor pulled her closer so she was pressed against him. They continued to kiss as Viktor's hand ran down her side and pulled up her dress and chemise. His hand trailed up her leg, over her ribbon garter holding her stocking up. Her hand went to his and she whispered, "should we be doing this? You are in mourning."

"I want too. You said Tamara would want to see me getting on with life." He pressed his lips against hers to silence her and pulled her into his crouch firmly with the hand on her buttocks.

She found herself panting even as she thought the situation all wrong. He was meant to be mourning his sister not having sex with her. She gave into it as she felt herself responding to the finger that was lazily stroking the crease between her buttocks, over the puckered hole and to the front, teasing her. Her free hand clung to his upper arm and she could feel his muscles from fencing practice under his shirt.

He smiled, enjoying hearing her panting and rubbing herself against his finger and penis. She murmured, "please."

"No." He fought his own urges. He wasn't sure when he would be able to see her again and wanted the moment to last as long as possible. They were two kindred souls joined together. How could God not see that? Why was he tearing them apart? The hand under their bodies moved up to cup the side of her face, his thumb exploring her face so he could remember it.

She kissed his thumb as it passed over her lips. She caught at it with her teeth as with her other hand she sought the buttons on his breeches. She wanted to feel him inside her so badly. She pushed him on to his back, lifted her dress and straddled him.

"What are you doing?"
She leant over and placed a finger on his lips, "ssh," before replacing it with her lips.

His hands clasped her buttocks and lifted her enough so she could find the tip of his erection. She slipped down it with a sigh of relief. His hands slipped up to her hips as she rode him. He stopped her, wanting her to beg and squirm, to grind into him till it became too much for one or both of them.

From the gentleness it had become filled with the harsh realities of unfulfilled needs. Their days were numbered. Neither knew that the other knew. It was something they had both chosen not to talk about.

She broke out of his grip and with one hand on his chest for balance she rode him hard. Maybe if she had a baby, a boy, they could be together forever but that would take nine months and he would be married by then! She began to cry silent tears as with a strangled groan from Viktor she made him come. She slowed, stopped and leant over to kiss him. He murmured, "I can't be without you."

"Don't go then. Stay."

"Koplev is waiting?"

"No." She lied. The servant would just have to camp out on the floor in the kitchen. She didn't want to let Viktor go though her mother may return at any moment.

"Any chance of a drink or food?"
She sat up with a laugh, "of course. Don't go anywhere." She slipped off him and the bed. He grabbed her arm, "but first…"
She smiled, expecting to be kissed.

"I really need to piss and," he blushed, "I can't do it on my own."

"I never…"

"You haven't needed to."

She pulled him towards her as she searched for her pisspot under the bed.

Viktor woke in the morning to Nastasia lying in his arms. He briefly thought he was dreaming. She had never stayed the night then he remembered he wasn't at home. He was at Nastasia's and he knew he couldn't stay. At some point, soon, they would find him missing. He had pretended to believe Nastasia's lie last night but he felt sure Koplev wouldn't have abandoned him. The servant would be out of work if he had.

He murmured in Nastasia's ear, "I have to go."

"Mmm…. It's not morning yet." She press her bottom into his crouch.

His hand swept up her naked body and squeezed her breast and felt her nipple react. He teased it between finger and thumb.

"Mmm." She sighed.

"Where's Koplev?"

"Probably asleep in the kitchen." She murmured, "mmm… Don't stop."

He leant over and kissed her cheek and slipped out of the bed. He remembered where she had placed his clothes the night before and reached for them with one hand on the bed so he kept his orientation of the room. Carefully he found the wall and then the door. He closed it behind him and called out in hushed tones, "Koplev? Koplev, are you here?"

"Sir?"

"Help me dress then let's head home."

"And Miss Balakina?

"Still asleep. I don't want to disturb her. Thank you Koplev."

"What for?"

"For everything."

Koplev grunted in reply as he helped Viktor dress by the light of his candle.

CHAPTER 16

Alla fretted. She'd gone to check on Viktor as her mother had requested, read from the Bible she had suggested. She hadn't expected to find his suite of rooms empty, furniture up ended. If she left her mother would know something was wrong so she waited instead. She put the furniture back in place, walked back and forth across the room and even sat in Viktor's chair by the fire wrapped in a blanket.

At some point she must have dozed off as she woke when the door creaked open to see Viktor entering from his bedroom in the early morning light. She rushed over to him and pulled him across the room and she hissed, "where have you been?!"

She backed up as she smelt the alcohol and sex on him, "were you with Nastasia Balakina?"

"So what if I was?"

"I've been protecting you from mother's wrath."

He dropped into his chair, "you didn't have to."

"What? And have the golden child appear as anything but that?" She retorted, her hands on her hips.

He put a hand to his head as the hangover kicked in, "go away Alla. And I'm not the golden child. Our brother was."

"Oh, you are. You and Tamara were. I played second fiddle to her and you, you…" the anger of how she was treated came out, "there's no dowry for me but you get all you want."

"No I don't."

"You are the eldest so even though you are blind, you are still the most important child."

"No I'm not. He was more important since he was going to be heir to whatever money we have which isn't much."

"Don't be foolish."

"I'm not. What we have is tied up in land and property. We have no money because the Empress hasn't paid us."

"What?" Alla sank on to the settle opposite him.

"We need Katerina's dowry. If we didn't then… then I wouldn't marry her. I am as much a slave to this family as you." He revealed. While on the estate his father had sat him down and told him of the situation their finances were in. That was why, however much he daydreamed about it, he knew he couldn't keep Nastasia. He **had** to marry Katerina "If I was a golden child would our mother hide me away?"

"It is the wounds, the scars…" She hesitantly said while she was still digesting everything Viktor had said. She whispered, "do you love Nastasia then?"
Viktor nodded.

"What are you going to do once you are married?"

"I don't know. I promised father it would come to an end before the wedding." He shrugged, "Alla?"

"Yes."

"It's just you and me now."

"Yes."

"I know you don't particularly like me."

"That's not true." She objected.

"Yes it is. You don't have to keep me company for much longer and I want you to get out there, find your friends and have some fun. Don't end up with a life like our aunt and her gossipy widows."

"I don't know."

"It's taken me long enough, don't wait so long. Just never call Nastasia a whore."

"I won't. Thank you Viktor." She crossed over and hugged him as tears welled up. He was right, he hadn't been the golden child. They had been more a like than she had ever realised, both trapped in the house but for different reasons.

Into her shoulder he said, "I know Tamara is dead. I know our mother tried to keep it from me. Can you take me to her grave so that I can say goodbye."
She leant back and smiled, "of course. We don't need her spirit haunting you."
That raised a small return smile from Viktor.

Alla accompanied Viktor to their sister's grave. She was glad they had spoken. She felt closer to him and felt he was giving her the chance to show she could be as good as Tamara. No longer was she under her elder sister's shadow. She knew she would never be her sister's equal, but Viktor had given her an olive branch and she had accepted it. Viktor noticed the difference the olive branch had done to his surviving sister as she tucked his hand into her elbow to lead him through the graveyard, past the rows of gravestones topped with orthodox crosses towards the Antipovs' new family plot.
They reached the mound of freshly turned earth that indicated Tamara's grave, "we are here."
"Can I have a few minutes alone?"
"Of course." She stepped away, leaving Viktor holding Borya's large collar. He pulled a silver rouble from his pocket and crouched before the grave. He dug out a small hole and put the coin in it, his contribution to helping Tamara on her way to standing before God. As he stood he said, "I never got a chance to say goodbye. He should have taken me, not you." He felt tears forming behind his mask, "I..."
He felt Alla's hand on his shoulder, "she would be glad that you are letting her go to be with God."
They heard a shout before Viktor could reply and they both looked in the direction of it. At Viktor's feet Borya growled.
Coming towards them was Gravil and his three

children making sure that the grave hadn't been disturbed and that her soul hadn't followed them back to the grave and had ascended to the Almighty's Presence. Seeing Viktor standing at Tamara's grave he declared, "you shouldn't be here. You don't deserve to be here. Get him away."

"Why?" Alla asked with a frown.

"You know perfectly well why."

"Let me remind you that he was closer to Tamara then you ever were. He is linked by blood while you are only so through marriage." She retorted fiercely to protect her brother's pride.

"He will not be seeing his niece and nephews."

"He has every right to." Alla objected.

"Alla, don't make a scene." Viktor pleaded and tried to draw his sister away. He had no wish for a scene at Tamara's graveside. She pulled her arm out of his hand and turned to glare at her brother-in-law properly. With hands on hips she protested, "you can't blame him for Tamara's death. It's not his fault he's blind. He's paid, we've all paid for his blindness. He doesn't deserve your anger. You should be blaming whoever caused the fire, not him."

"Alla..."

"Ssh Viktor." She snapped at him and then looked to Gravil again, still glaring. The man scowled and then turned as to his children he commanded, "come."

"But uncle Viktor?" Ilya piped up.

"Silence Ilya. You will not be seeing him ever again. He's a bad man."

"Why?" Lev asked with concern.

"He killed your mother."

Lev stopped walking and turned to look at his uncle with wide eyes.

"They are walking away aren't they?" Viktor remarked quietly.

"They are." Alla answered but then saw Lev running towards them.

Lev ran towards his uncle, ignoring his father's shout to return to his side. He embraced his uncle. Viktor put a hand on the boy's head and asked, "who is it?"

"It's Lev, uncle. Father isn't right. You aren't bad."

"Thank you Lev, but perhaps you should go now." He smiled down at his nephew, "I don't want you to get in trouble with your father."

There were heavy, angry steps as Gravil came to claim his son. He shouted, "Lev, get here now!"

"When I am a man I will get in contact somehow." Viktor smiled again, "I think you'd best go."

Lev looked up at his uncle's masked face and then ran back to his father who slapped him round the head in anger. Lev glanced back, hand on his ear, as he followed his father.

Alla and Viktor remained a little longer but the atmosphere had changed because of Gravil. At Viktor's wish she led him back to the carriage.

"I should thank you for standing up for me. I didn't expect it."

"We only have each other now remember. We'll support each other?"

"Yes."

She smiled to herself as they walked.

CHAPTER 17

Two days before the wedding Viktor couldn't delay it any longer. He sent for Nastasia. She kissed him once she arrived, "hello handsome."

"You are in a good mood." He observed knowing he was about to shatter the mood.

"Yes I am."

"Please, I need you to sit down." He cautiously said.

"Oh? What's wrong Viktor?" She became worried. She had a feeling she knew what was coming since he was soon to be married. She could only hope it was actually going to be an apartment, or maybe just a few rooms.
He cleared his throat, "as you know I am to be wed in the next few days. I made a promise to my father that I would give you up once I was wed."
He paused and wished he could see Nastasia's reaction. She didn't say anything. She held her breath waiting to see which way the conversation would go.

"I do not want to lose you." He gulped nervously, "I must give you up. I respect my father too much to ignore the promise I made."

"He doesn't need to know; she doesn't need to know." She found herself kneeling at his feet and holding tight to his knee as she pleaded, "I could find an apartment and then you could visit me. Please, I don't want you to give me up."

"I have to. You'll find another man to support you."

"No!" She shouted, "no! I don't want to. I don't want to be another man's. I only want to be yours. Marry me, not Katerina."

"You are just a whore like your mother and no one marries a whore." He snapped. He had to drive her away somehow, "I've used you and you've used me and now it's time for us to go our separate ways."

"I have not used you." She protested, "I wanted to be with you and I know you feel the same." She got to her feet, "you are a poor liar Viktor Tverdislavich Medevdev."

"I want to thank you for making me a man." He reached for a slim cloth wrapped box on his side table. Finding it he held it out for Nastasia to take.

She knocked it out of his hand. She didn't want to be bought off again. She didn't want to go back to her mother's and get mocked for not being able to keep the attentions of a man. She didn't want to find herself being dragged deeper into the life of a mistress. She didn't want to find herself with an ugly old man that her mother would find for her. She said, "you are a monster Viktor, just like you have always thought. A spoilt brat of a monster." She ran from the room.

Viktor sat stunned. He hadn't expected that reaction. Had he just lost more than a lover? Had he lost the closest thing to a best friend? What would she do in revenge to him abandoning her? He could only hope she wouldn't do anything.

He felt tears welling up and hastily rubbed them away. Already he was missing her. He wanted to call her back and apologise. He drew in a deep breath to steady his emotions before speaking to Koplev who he knew was in the room., "make sure she gets it."

"Yes sir."

"Bring me something strong to drink."

"Yes sir."

She walked the streets until her rage had cooled under the rain. She didn't want to face her mother. With reluctance she returned home but only because she needed to dry out. As she entered the apartment her mother called out, "Nastasia?"

With a sigh she responded, "yes mother?"

"I'm glad you are back. You have a visitor."

"Oh?" She became hopeful. Had Viktor come to apologise and admit he couldn't do without her. She hurried in and came to a stop when she saw Katerina. Katerina sat opposite Valentina Balakina and blushed uncomfortably while clasping her tea. Stiffly Nastasia asked, "what do you want?"

"Darling, you are soaking wet." Her mother observed, "what have you being doing? I thought you were seeing Viktor?"

Katerina hastily stood, "let me help you get changed." Nastasia didn't respond to either of them as she retreated to her bedroom where she instructed a maid to get hot water and towels and help her undress.

Katerina excused herself from her father's mistress' tedious conversation. She lingered in Nastasia's bedroom door. Nastasia glanced across, "what do you want? Are you here to mock me?"

"No." Katerina found her voice, "I was hoping for some advice?"

"Why should I? You are the one who ended our friendship and you are the one who has now driven Viktor away from me." Nastasia pointed out bitterly.

Katerina could have argued back that actually her half sister had taken Viktor from her but that would not have helped her. She couldn't look her half sister in the eye, "I have no one else to turn to."

Seeing that her half-sister was scared Nastasia capitulated. She was going to need Katerina again to survive an otherwise lonely life. She wrapped a robe around herself as with a sigh she sat on her bed, "go on then."

Cautiously Katerina sat down beside her half sister. She picked at a loose thread on her skirt as she found the courage to ask the questions she had. Finding the courage she needed she blurted out, "what's it like?"

"What's what like?" Nastasia asked with a frown.
Katerina blushed, "sex?"
Nastasia snorted a laugh.

"I want to make Viktor happy." Katerina went on. Nastasia debated whether to be vindictive or not before saying bluntly, "just lie back and spread your legs. That's all you need to do. Leave the pleasure to others."

"Oh?" Katerina's face fell and she nervously asked, "does it hurt?" She fiddled with the skirt of her dress.

"At first." Nastasia admitted.

"Do you enjoy it?" Katerina asked with curiosity.

"Yes." Nastasia smiled to herself at some of the things she and Viktor had got up to. She studied the nervous Katerina and came up with an idea, "you know, if you don't like it, you can always send Viktor to me."
Katerina's back straightened and she raised her head, "no thank you. I will learn to enjoy it."
Nastasia's head lowered, and her shoulders sagged. She had tried.
Trying to be reconciliatory Katerina suggested, "you can always come to the dinner, it's open doors."
Nastasia looked up in shock, "what?! And have you mock me, no thanks. I think it's time you left."
Katerina realised she had stretched Nastasia goodwill as far as it would go and knew it was time to go. She stood as she tentatively said, "thank you for your advice."

The door to the apartment opened and closed as Katerina left. Nastasia breathed a sigh of relief, now she could be alone. But it wasn't to be as her mother appeared at the door holding a cloth wrapped gift, "this came for you as well."

"I don't want it. He's trying to pay me off since he no

longer wants me."

"What do you mean?" Her mother frowned with concern.

"It's over because he is marrying the bitch that has just left and all she wanted was to know how to please him herself." Nastasia spat before starting to cry.

"Oh dear. You're going to have to develop a wall round that heart of yours. Our life doesn't get to end like the tales of princes and princesses. We never get the prince, but we do get the fun." Valetina Balakina sat down beside her daughter. She put an arm round Nastasia, "you've learnt your second lesson. Never fall in love with the man who pays for your keep. Did you tell her anything?"

"No, no." Nastasia stammered.

"Good; then he might come back. Now let's see what he got you. Even if you never wear it this is your protection for when you might need money."

Nastasia shrugged, she didn't care, she just wanted Viktor back.

Her mother's eyes lit up with excitement at what expensive jewellery might be in the box but it quickly became disappointment though what was on her lap was still beautiful.

Wrapped in the cloth there was a Muscovite painted icon of the Saints Peter and Fervonica with gold leaf haloes. Bearded Peter stood in his richly coloured gown and cloak with one arm around Fervoncia who was equally well dressed. She held a dove in her hands. Before Valentina were a pair of lovers who stayed together, peasant and noble, even as St Peter's Boyars disagreed with their marriage. They were sent away but when the Boyars couldn't agree on who would be their new Prince they invited the saints back and peace returned to their city home of Murom. She healed him of his leprosy. Was Viktor suggesting she had healed him? The bit all lovers of romance liked was that they died on the same day in their separate monastic homes and though they were buried separately they were found together, a miracle!

Valentina sighed. All women knew the story and dreamed of a love like the two saints. Perhaps Nastasia wouldn't appreciate the gift just yet but she saw the meaning behind it.

The tears had stopped and she saw her daughter looking at it. Nastasia looked at the icon and realised that Viktor was telling her that he hadn't wanted to give her up. Maybe he was promising that he wouldn't let his family keep them apart forever. She decided to live with that hope however fragile it would become. She would pray to them and see if her wish came true.

CHAPTER 18

There was lots of giggling amongst the young women around Katerina. There were a few friends from court and the rest were all family members. They plaited her hair like the serfs did to encourage fertility. They then tied her crest shaped kokoshnik headdress on. It was embroidered with pearls and plant and flower motifs in gold on a red background. The wide ribbons trailed down her back, over the white dress which had silver asters, lilies and fern flowers and leaves woven into the fabric. Her father had spoilt her as his only daughter. They covered her headdress and head in a long silk organza veil embroidered by herself with the same flowers on her dress to bless the marriage with love and fertility. A friend remarked, "he'll have to watch no one tries to steal you away."

"I don't want that happening." Katerina said with a frown.

"Why ever not?"

"You know why?"

"Spoilsport. Now, no frowning." Her friend pouted.

They heard horses outside and ran to the windows leaving Katerina playing nervously with the edge of her veil. One of her nieces called back, "they are here."

"It's too late now. What shall we demand of him?" A cousin asked, turning round to look at the bride.

"Please don't." Katerina said as she lifted her veil. She carefully crossed the room to look down at the carriages and men on horseback. She saw Viktor sitting straight backed in the carriage dressed in dark blue and silver with a matching mask and wondered if he was as nervous as she was.

"Come on, it's tradition." The cousin pleaded.

"We are not Cossacks who need to steal their bride or demand ransoms. We are of noble birth Elena."

"Fine." Elena sighed reluctantly.

It was a parade of wealth that headed through the streets of St Petersburg to the church with the bride and groom hidden inside their carriage to deter evil spirits. They rode in silence, Katerina staring at her hands clasped in her lap. She wondered if other couples were like the two of them. She glanced up and looked through her veil at Viktor. His mask hid any sense of what he might be thinking. Their last conversation had ended badly but she had to try, "Viktor?"
He didn't move.

He was doing this because his family had decided so, but it didn't mean he had to make polite conversation with his bride. Thoughts were on Nastasia, would she be at the church or the party? Did she understand the meaning behind his last gift? For the moment he would do his duty and try and turn his thoughts away from Nastasia. He ignored Katerina's tentative attempt to make conversation. He was relieved to feel the carriage slow down. He stepped out and held out his hand for her.

Once in the church the bride and groom walked up to the altar holding a candle each, Viktor's hand tucked into Katerina's elbow. They held the candles throughout the ceremony as prayers and blessings were made. Crowns, made of silver and decorated with stylised foliage and cartouches with two arches met with a cross atop an orb at the top of the crown, were placed on their heads by the priest as he said three times, "the servant of God, Viktor Tverdislavich Medevdev, is crowned to handmaid of God Katerina Livovna Kolesova; in the name of the Father, and the Son and of the Holy Spirit. The handmaid of God, Katerina Livovna Kolesova is crowned to the servant of God, Viktor Tverdislavich Medevdev. Amen."
The crowns, tied together with ribbon were switched between the couple as the priest chanted, "O Lord, our

God, crown them with glory and honour."

They both took three sips from the common cup before being led round the altar while the choir sang to the Holy Martyrs. They received a final blessing each, "be thou magnified O Bridegroom, as Abraham, and blessed as Isaac and multiply as Jacob. Walk in peace and work in righteousness, as the commandments of God." He blessed Viktor with the sign of the cross. To Katerina he said, "and thou O Bride, be though magnified as Sarah, glad as Rebecca and multiply like unto Rachel, rejoicing in thine own husband, fulfilling the conditions of the law, for so it is well pleasing unto God."
The audience exclaimed, "*Na Zisete*," as the priest made the sign of the cross over Katerina.

The wedding party went back to the Kolesovs' house where the windows and doors were shut to keep any evil spirit away. Considering his blindness the elders of the Kolesov family didn't want any malevolent spirits to attach themselves to the new couple and cause the same affliction in the next generation though they knew he hadn't been born so. But they said amongst themselves 'you could never be too careful with these sorts of things.'

With silent giggles Alla and Elena stood at the entrance with the small loaf of bread which would bless the couple and determine who would be in charge. As the bride and groom entered the bread was offered to them, "let's see who will rule the family. Close your eyes and no hands." Blushing Katerina lifted her veil and closed her eyes. Obediently the newly married couple opened their mouths.

Alla and Elena looked at each other and broke the loaf in half and together shoved their halves in the couple's mouths. They laughed as the couple struggled to close their mouths. Elena decreed cheekily, "they will be equals. Let them love and fight in equal measure."

Those closest laughed at the sight while those further back cheered.

"Now let the celebrating begin." Liv Antonovich called out, beaming at his blushing daughter.

Katerina and Viktor led the way to the dining room where the tables were laid with the finest china, cutlery, glasses and food. It wasn't the only room. Another room was laid with plainer china and cutlery for those who came from the Count's business connections and anyone else who wanted to enjoy the generosity of a family celebrating a marriage.

The feasting went on most of the day and then finally those who were sober enough led the couple to the Medevdevs' house for the bedding of the new couple. Viktor was feeling on the drunk side from so many toasts of strong Polish vodka as well as wine. Katerina had eaten very little from nerves at what was to come.

Elena helped Katerina undress while Koplev did his master. Before she knew it silence descended on Viktor's suite of rooms. She watched Koplev help Viktor towards the bed and remembered what the Countess had said to her earlier, "he is fragile and will always need lots of care."

At the time she had thought Daria drunk and been sceptical based on what she had seen of him but now she wasn't so sure.

From the bed she looked round the plainly decorated room, trying not to be embarrassed by the man getting into bed beside her. On the fireplace's mantle, reflected in the mirror was the bridal candle. Other candelabras lit up the bed and its occupants. On a table was a plate of cold meats, cheese and rye bread for if they got hungry plus a decanter of watered wine and two glasses. Finally she looked at Viktor in his night shirt as Koplev disappeared into his tiny bedroom next door. He sat back against his pillows.

"So…?" She tried to break the tense silence between them. She pulled her knees up under the blankets and hugged them. She felt chilly though it was warm.
He cleared his throat, "you probably should know something about my blindness."
He pulled off his mask and Katerina gasped in shock at the sight of the top half of his face. A part of her wanted to order him to put the mask back on. His one eye stared blankly not quite in her direction while the glass eye horrified her. Then there was the scarring which puckered the skin and made his torn left eyelid stand out. Cautiously she asked, "can I touch it?"

"If you want but be careful as it still hurts at times."

She knelt on the bed and hesitantly touched one of his scars. He reached up and put his hand on hers. She asked, "how did it happen?"

"We used to have a bear on the estate and it attacked me. So, now you know, what do you think of me?"

"As I promised I'll look after you and be the best wife I can be." She said with a tight smile, "I hope in time we can grow to love each other."

"Maybe." Thoughts of Nastasia came to the forefront of his mind.

"What do we do now? I know everyone is expecting us to consummate our marriage."

"I'm going to sleep." He yawned and slid down into bed.

She was disappointed and relieved as he turned his back on her. She lay down herself, on her back, and gazed up at the ceiling. Would he turn to her and do the deed expected? She lay tensely waiting until she heard him softly snoring and only then did she let herself fall asleep.

She woke early, feeling hot and disorientated. It took her a moment to work out who was lying beside her in a strange bed, in a strange bedroom. Then she remembered she was a married woman and beside her was her husband, a man hat looked more like a *upior* than a man. She shuddered and was glad he wasn't facing her way. She wondered what Nastasia had seen in him. She briefly debated with herself about letting her friend keep him and then told herself off for even thinking that.

She rubbed tired eyes as she hadn't slept well. She worried what the families would say if the marriage wasn't consummated. She slipped out of bed and crossed to the windows. She looked out and saw the first rays of dawn and sighed. There would be more celebrating today. She crossed back to the bed and murmured, "Viktor? Do you think we could sneak away and go for a walk in the Summer Garden instead?"

"Come back to bed." He turned in bed. He felt the bed move as she got back into it. He ordered, "take off your nightgown."

"Why?"

"Because I want you to." He answered sternly. He had sobered up and now it was time to show his family and Katerina that he was a man, "I have yet to learn your body which before God is now mine."

Obediently she removed her nightdress and lay down and lay still as she didn't know what he would do. She watched as he moved towards her and remembered what Nastasia had said and spread her legs for him. She watched with wide eyes as he straddled her legs, drawing them together and trapping her.

He bent over her and his fingers began to explore her hair and then her face, moving over her nose and slightly open mouth. They continued down her body and he found himself starting to compare her to Nastasia. Katerina's breasts were smaller, her stomach flatter and her hips felt narrower. He found her coarse wiry pubic hair, the symbol of her womanhood, untouched by man's trespassing fingertips until now. She would not be keeping her virginity for much longer. He felt her tense as his hand went further between her thighs.

As he sat up she looked down the length of her body and spotted his erection, swollen and its veins pulsing. She closed her eyes and gulped. She was relieved when he leant over her again. Nothing anyone had joked about had warned her of how hideous it looked, almost as bad as his scarring. She opened her eyes when she felt his fingers on her now quivering lip. His face drew closer to hers and then he was kissing her. She relaxed a little. To her a kiss was safe. She became wary again as his lips moved over her throat and down to her breasts.

A hand went back between her tights. She let out a gasp as his fingers probed her and then slipped into her. With a knee he parted her thighs. She murmured, "please be gentle Viktor, I've never done this."

"I know." He said as he sat up. He guided himself into her. He nudged into her as he could feel how tight she was. The next thrust went all the way in and she let out a cry of pain and shock. She closed her eyes against Viktor's hideous rocking face above hers. She turned her head so she didn't have to smell the stale alcohol on his breath.

He came quickly and lay on her before rolling off. He remarked without emotion, "it will get easier."

"Viktor?"

"Mmm?" He responded sleepily.

"Will it always hurt?"

"Don't think so."

"Will you show me what you like?" She cautiously asked as she tried to ignore the semen and blood dribbling out of her.

"I will certainly show you. Now, quiet." He dozed off.

They got up a few hours later for the second day of celebrating. The maids moved in as soon as the couple had

gone with Koplev overseeing them with the Countess'
maid. One of the maids remarked, "his second one. How
many more will bloody these sheets I wonder?"

"Quiet. Was the deed done?" The Countess' maid
demanded.

"There's your proof." The maid threw back the blankets
to show the blood on the sheet, "he can clearly do it though
he can't see."

"Hmpfh." Koplev, his arms crossed, expressed with
warning that the maid was talking out of turn.

"I'll go tell Her Ladyship." The elder maid said and swept
from the room.

"Get this bed changed quickly." Koplev ordered before
also leaving the room.
The two young maids stuck their tongues out at the closed
door and one remarked, "stuck up bitch and bastard."

"Come on, we are going to have to soak this sheet." The
other said as she began pulling the sheet off.

Katerina was thrilled to receive a personal invite to
the palace considering she had only been included on her
father's invites under 'and family' until now. She dressed to
impress in green silk and with the emerald jewellery
hanging from her ears and round her throat. She chose for
Viktor the same colour and saw Daria's look of disbelief as
they came down the stairs.

Katerina was no longer just a daughter, she was a
wife, a woman in her own right. She had seen Viktor was
more than capable of looking after himself and she didn't
have to play nursemaid as she thought. Now she got to
enjoy the freedom of being a wife. She was also determined
to keep the claws of her half-sister away from her new
husband. Seeing the look Katerina smiled ruefully, Viktor
was now her's. Viktor and his father were oblivious to the
power struggle going on.

They all travelled together in the carriage to the Peterhof for the afternoon ball, Borya spread across their feet panting. When they reached the palace with everyone else Viktor allowed Katerina to lead them through the other courtiers though one hand was on Borya's large collar. They walked through the rooms and out into the gardens where musicians were playing. Katerina broke away when she saw her friends leaving Viktor to be led by Borya along a path following an interesting scent.

He didn't know where he was going but a complaining roar of an animal froze him to the spot. Laughter followed as members of the court watched a brown bear dancing to the beat of the drum, a chain attached to a ring in its nose. The back of its hind legs were scarred from being beaten by sticks to make it dance.

He felt fear worming its way up from his feet and up his legs, pinning him to the spot. He didn't know whether it would come any closer. He was sent back to when he was ten and the family's bear attacked him. He had been teasing it, poking it with a stick to make it dance. He knew he shouldn't have been there without the bear keeper but he was the important son and believed he could do whatever he wanted. He had laughed with success as the juvenile brown bear rose up on to its hind legs. He had stopped when it swatted the stick away and then the next swipe had been across his eyes.

He came back to the present as he felt Borya's wet nose in his hand but then it was gone. With a bark Borya ran towards the bear and leapt at it. There were cries of shock and then the men started betting as the dancing bear entertainment became a bear baiting. There were snarls and roars as the two animals fought.

He felt someone brush past his arm and take his hand, "Who is there?"

"It's your sister."

“Alla?” He exclaimed in relief and then in fear, “where's the bear?”

“Far enough away that you will not be harmed.”

“Are you sure?”

“Certain. Come on, let's get you inside.”
He nodded and let his sister lead him into the palace and to a quiet side chamber. She asked as she pressed him into a chair, “shall I stay and keep you company.”

“I'll be fine, but thank you.” He produced a small tight smile.

“I'll go find Katerina.” She squeezed his shoulder before leaving.

Katerina rushed to Viktor's side as soon as Alla told her what had happened. She dropped to her knees and took his hand, “forgive me husband, if I had known.”

“Katerina?” He was startled to hear her asking for forgiveness.

“I should have stayed at your side.”

“That wasn't necessary.”

“Sir? Madam?” Another voice entered the conversation, the voice of a slightly nervous servant.

“Yes?” Viktor responded.

“Apologies but your dog is now dead. What should we do would with the body?”

“Dispose of it. I don't want it.”

“Viktor?!” Katerina protested, “what about the years of obedience it has given you?”

“Do as I say.” Viktor snapped as he sensed the servant hesitating. He directed to Katerina, “I don't want to hear your opinion.” He would mourn privately later over his canine companion.

The servant left, with a bow towards the man who entered. Viktor recognised the footsteps, “father?”
The Count looked between husband and wife with a frown, “what's going on here?”

"Borya just got himself killed fighting a bear." Viktor remarked without emotion while a tear ran down Katerina's cheek from being told off as well as being upset over the sudden death of Borya.

"Oh."

"I want to go home Katerina." Viktor remarked, "you can stay if you want. This isn't the place for me."

"Oh." She sounded disappointed and relieved. She wondered whether he would go and seek solace with Nastasia and a tiny part of her, which she quickly squashed, hoped he would.

"I'm done here Viktor so you can come with me." His father offered as he glanced between the young couple, trying to work out what was going on between them. He cleared his throat to say something and then thought better of it. They would find their way just as Daria and he had. Viktor held out a hand and Katerina took it. He kissed it before saying stiffly, "enjoy the rest of your day and then come home and tell me all about it."

She nodded numbly and watched as father and son walked away. She took a deep breath of relief, straightened her back and walked back into the palace to find her friends. She would show the world that she could still be herself without her husband present. She wasn't going to let herself become known as the wife of the man with the mask. She wanted to be her own person.

CHAPTER 19

Nastasia hoped that seven days had been enough time for Viktor to realise how much he missed her. Only if he didn't respond would she submit to the attentions of one of the men who were already sniffing around her much to her mother's excitement.

She arrived at the servant's entrance and asked for Koplev. When he arrived she asked, "is Katerina Livonva in?"

He looked sorry for her and she shuffled her feet with embarrassment. She didn't want to come across needy but probably did.

"She is out."

She released the breath she had been holding, "can I see Viktor?"

"Are you sure?" He asked with concern.

"Please. I… I just need to talk with him."

Koplev looked at the young woman before him and really did feel sorry for her. She had been good for Viktor, brought him out of his shell, brought him to life, had made him calmer. All that had gone when he had let her go. He didn't know about Nastasia but Viktor had moped until the day of the wedding. Even now he was quieter. Katerina hadn't had the same affect on him. Just this morning he had heard them arguing. He knew he wasn't going to be able to dissuade her and sternly said, "don't blame me for anything he says."

Nastasia hesitated in the doorway then stepped in, "I had to come and congratulate you on your marriage." She had been at their feasts but hadn't dared approach them. She had watched from a distance so as not to direct evil spirits towards them as she wished it was her who had just married him, not Katerina. She had hoped to speak to him but the preening, smiling bitch never left his side and in the end she had retreated home to cry.

"Nastasia?" He asked in surprise, "what are you doing here?"

She sensed his uncertainly and took it. She ran across the room and knelt at his feet, "I have missed you."

He hesitated and sought the hand she had placed on his knee. With a long sigh he admitted, "I have as well."

"I could be your lover again." She shyly suggested.

His facial expression showed pain. He wanted to but he had made a promise and his marriage was only seven days old. He needed to give Katerina a chance. With reluctance he said, "I can't."

"Can't?"

"It would not be fair on Katerina." He tried to keep his voice empty of emotion.

"But you don't love her." Damn his blindness for his eyes wouldn't be able to lie to her. She felt his hand tighten around hers and smiled, he could pretend all he wanted but his grip had revealed what he really thought.

"I can't. You should go before Katerina returns."

"Where is she?" Nastasia demanded, "she's left you on your own."

"She keeps my bed warm."

Nastasia jerked her head in shock at his statement. That was the worst excuse she had ever heard for anything but she ran with it, "I can keep your bed warm as well. I can give you a warm and welcoming bed, better than her."

"I need to try." His lips pressed tight together and pulled back his hand so he wouldn't lean forward and seek out and kissed her familiar lips. She wouldn't release it.

"But she doesn't make you happy like I do." Her voice was tight as she suppressed an urge to wail out her protest. He squeezed her hand as he softly said, "I can't."

Nastasia fought back the tears as she got to her feet. With a gulp she said, "I hope you and Katerina have a good life." She made it halfway to the door before turning and running to him. She held his face and kissed him hard. She broke away and ran from the room leaving Viktor touching his lips where moments ago her lips had been. He slammed a fist on to the table, knocking over the jug on it. Damn God! Damn Katerina! Damn his parents! He wanted Nastasia so badly and couldn't have her.

He snapped at Koplev when his servant entered an hour later, "What is it?" He paused and then reluctantly added, "don't ever let Nastasia in again."

"Of course." Koplev replied without emotion.

"What do you want anyway?"

"I have a message from the palace, from Orianenbaum. It seems Grand Duke Peter Fredorovitch wishes to see you."

"Me?"

Koplev stood in silence. All he had done was pass on the message.

"When?"

"Tomorrow. He's only interested in you, no one else."

"You'd best come with me."

"Yes sir."

The Grand Duke was thrashing around a sabre in the courtyard of the fort he had had built for his Holstein regiment. It was a complete little town on the Orianenbaum estate with a Lutheran church, office buildings and barracks for the regiment all within a 12 pointed star shaped defences. A group of young men and woman stood near by talking, staying out of the way of the sharp sword. A line of Holstein soldiers dressed in their blue coats with either yellow or white waistcoats stood to one side. White belts diagonally crossed their chests and swords hung at their sides. Cupped into their hands and leaning against their shoulders were their muskets. The six men stood on display as the heir to the Russian throne shouted at them.

The tall thin young man dressed in matching uniform, stopped swinging his sword as he heard Viktor's and Koplev's footsteps. He turned with a big grin, "aah, you have come, excellent. Look everyone." He called to the group who approached with curiosity, "I have heard that this blind man can use a sword as well as any man who can see. What do you think?"
There was tittering from the group as they eyed Viktor who held tight to the top of his new cane with Koplev a few steps behind him.

Viktor shifted and felt his cheeks beginning to warm up. He may not be able to see those staring at him but could definitely hear the disdain and mocking tone in the heir's voice and his companions. He took a deep breath as he wondered whether he should have come at all if he was going just an amusement for the rulers of Russia. He bowed in the direction of the voices, "your Highness, thank you for the invite."

"Yes, yes… whatever." The Grand Duke waved a hand dismissively, "now, can you actually fence?"

"Yes sir."

"How were you blinded? Were you a soldier?"

"Err…" Viktor was hesitant, "no sir, it was a bear when I was younger."

"And you survived?"

"Yes sire."

"That is incredible, isn't it?" The Grand Duke looked back at his entourage.

They spoke their affirmations.

He turned back to his guest as he gestured for someone to step forward and receive instructions, "find him a sword and Konrad. I want to see if he really is as good as I have

148

heard whispered."

Koplev stepped forward and murmured, "you don't have to do this." He didn't think the Countess would want Viktor putting himself at risk for the amusement of others. Viktor waved his own hand dismissively. He didn't like how he was being spoken of and was going to show them all that he was not to be underestimated. The duel with Ivan had shown that. Had word got out about it for the Grand Duke to be showing an interest?

He shrugged off his coat and handed it to Koplev. He then pulled off his mask. Nastasia had shown him the scars were nothing to be embarrassed about. If she didn't care about them then why should he still be ashamed of them. Let strangers make up their own stories, only a few would ever know it was from being a brat as a child.

It took a moment for his eye to focus on the group before him. He saw one shape in a dress react to the sight of his scars. He saw them turn as someone new approached the group.

Approaching was a young man dressed in the Holstein uniform but holding his hat. A sword bounced at his hip and another was in his hand. He clicked his heels together and bowed to Grand Duke Peter Fredorovitch, "sire."

"Excellent. You are going to challenge Viktor Tverdislavich Medevdev here to a sparring match."
The officer looked at Viktor and frowned, "can he even see?"

"I can see enough." Viktor replied stiffly, "hand me the sword and I will show you." He held out a hand.
A smile spread across the Prussian's face. He was up for the challenge. He was tempted to throw the rapier to see what reflex reactions Viktor had but decided to be the gentleman he was and held it out.

With the sword in his hand he judged the weight of

it and adjusted his stance. The way this was going he wasn't expecting it to be carried out under fair or gentlemanly rules. His one eye watched his shadowy opponent as he in turn waited for a cue from the Grand Duke.

The Duke whispered in the ear of one of his courtiers who then approached the Holstein solder and passed on the message. The Prussian looked at Viktor and smiled ruthlessly. He glanced over the Grand Duke who gave him a curt nod.

The Viktor could sense the tension in the air and braced himself for the attack. He saw the rapier coming towards him and lifted his own in defence.

They parried back and forth, neither one giving much ground to the other. They fought with sharp blades and Viktor winced as he felt his opponent's blade slice through his shirt and upper arm. He heard the women gasp.

His head lifted as he heard footsteps from behind him. Instinct told him that he was about to go up against another. He spun round and thrust his blade in front of him and felt it get jerked sideways. He wanted to object but didn't dare. He wanted to win to prove himself. Prove himself to who though? He let out a few stressed puffs of breath. His now two opponents were moving too much for his poor sight to cope and the warm day wasn't helping either. If only they would stop moving so he could orientate himself. Their tread was too similar for him to keep track of them.

He forced himself to standstill which made the two Holstein soldiers hesitate and glance at each other, wondering whether they should continue to attack. Viktor closed his eye so he could concentrate on his other senses. He felt the warm salty breeze off the sea. He heard the audience talking and could smell the sweat of the two soldiers. He knew then that he wasn't going to win but he had to put on a performance to ensure the Grand Duke was amused. Gossip said he could be volatile. If he had known what he was getting into he would have politely declined if that was even possible to do to your rulers.

He lifted a hand to rub sweat off his forehead. He heard a woman say, "enough Peter. You don't need to torment the poor man. He's not a toy to play with."

"I don't have to listen to you." The Grand Duke replied with disdain "I didn't invite you so you can bugger back off."

"Why are you interested in him anyway?"
The Grand Duke laughed, "ha! Look at him, the fool, he's nothing but a freak." He gestured over at Viktor, "I admit he's good at fencing but he's no good for anything else. He can't call himself a man. He'll never be a soldier."

Viktor's free hand became a fist while the other gripped the sword even tighter. He felt humiliated. He felt a hand on his shoulder and Koplev's voice close to his ear, "start walking backwards. It is the Grand Duchess. They are all watching them argue or trying there best not to." Viktor carefully nodded and allowed his manservant to lead him slowly backwards.
Koplev glared at the two Holstein soldiers, warning them off saying anything. One just shrugged, the other nodded in acknowledgement. Yes Viktor wouldn't have won against them both but he had put up a good fight.

As Viktor climbed into his carriage they heard footsteps and turned, "Viktor Tverdislavich?"

"Yes?" Viktor replied warily.

"You come back here another time. We not like the Grand Duke." The Holstein solider said in poor Russian, "you good with sword. Must share."
Koplev put his hand on Viktor but it was shaken off.

"Yes."

"Good food, drink, practice?"

"Yes."

"Send message?"

"Yes." Viktor smiled, excited at the thought of hanging out with like minded men.

Koplev cleared his throat. Viktor ignored his servant's hints of concern.

Viktor couldn't help grinning as they arrived back at the family's St Petersburg home. It didn't matter that he was going to lose badly, it had been exhilarating, out showing he could do something other than sitting in the house. His mother appeared in the entrance hall and demanded, "where have you been?"

The ear-to-ear grin disappeared, "out." He looked behind and added sternly to his servant, "don't you dare tell her Koplev."

"Koplev?!" She turned to the servant and threatened, "I can get rid of you quite easily."

Koplev shrugged rebelliously. He knew he was safe as they wouldn't ever find anyone else. He replied, "out."

"Where is your mask?"

Viktor shrugged, "does it matter now? You are the only one embarrassed about it."

"Viktor," Daria changed tack, "you look sweaty and feverish. You must be behaving like this because you are ill. Perhaps we should leave the city for a few days, go to the dacha."

"Mother, I am not ill." He objected as his mother placed a hand on his face. He fought the urge to push his mother away.

"Yes. You are feverish. Whatever you were doing has unbalanced you." She tried to sound concerned but Viktor could hear through it to the tone of 'I know my son best'.

And that is how he ended up lying under a tree with

Katerina, his mother in a chair nearby. They were all causal dressed in loose shirts and trousers and simple but quality sarafans. He wasn't going to admit it but the peace of the garden was good, feeling the sun on his face except Katerina didn't like him not wearing a mask. It made him miss Nastasia. He would have been able to tell her about the encounter with the Grand Duke and the invitation to return to the barracks. He was waiting for such an invite now. He hadn't even tried telling Katerina, she wasn't interested in his only interest. She was often out leaving him on his own anyway.

Katerina sat under the shade of the tree in the garden of the family's Dacha. Viktor lay beside her on the blanket with his silvery blonde haired head resting in her lap. It was too hot to do anything but doze in the hazy sunlight. He slept with his shirt undone while her bodice was loose against the heat. Sweat dripped down her cleavage.

She softly stroke his hair, thankful that he slept under his mask. She had tried to do what he liked but hated it. She hadn't liked holding his erection and hadn't liked being on top of him. She didn't find sex enjoyable. Most of the time she lay there waiting for it to be over. She couldn't understand how Nastasia put up with Viktor's scarred face. How could she want to have sex with him leering down at her?

She had prayed hard to God for herself to become pregnant so that he would leave her be. In the last few days she had come to realise she had missed another bleeding. She now feared the eight months to come.

Feeling the Countess' eyes on her she looked up. The older woman sat in her chair with Alla close by. Daria had never seen him sleep like he did now, even after being worn out from playing. He had refused to sleep against her or his nursemaid. Those few summers after he had been

153

blinded had been painful and carefree as the children had adapted and only she had been embarrassed by her son's appearance. He had sensed her discomfort and that had been the start of his fits when he fought the masks being put on.

With a rare smile of kindness towards her daughter-in-law she remarked, "you have a magic touch. He would never sleep like that with me."
Katerina blushed, "thank you, but I think it is the heat. It is making me drowsy as well."
"He trusts you Katerina."
Katerina didn't contradict the Countess. She wasn't going to admit they lived as a reluctant couple. She had her social life that kept her busy but she knew it couldn't stay like that. At some point they would be forced together and then the fireworks would start again. He didn't want her or need her and she knew it. She felt sure he still thought of Nastasia and as for herself she felt like second best. She thought she would be happy being married but didn't feel it especially when under Viktor at night.

The Countess eyed her and asked, "have you something to tell me?"
"What do you mean?" Katerina looked worried.
"You have not bled for two months." The Countess said sternly.
Katerina looked shocked, how did her mother in law know?
"Well?"
Katerina gulped, "I think I am."
"Good. You must pray for a boy."
"Yes madam." She meekly bowed her head.
"You must let Viktor know. Tell him this evening." Daria ordered as she smiled in triumphant, "then there will be no more intimate moments. The baby must not be disturbed in your womb."

She obeyed the Countess' ordered suggestion and led Viktor through the Dacha's garden that was aspiring to be French. The perfumes from the flowers rose around them in the evening's warmth. A breeze swirled the fragrance around the couple. Silently they walked down the path.

Viktor allowed her to lead him along the paths. He held out his free hand which brushed over the flowers. He finally spoke, "you have been quiet this evening. Is there something on your mind?"

She looked up at his masked face while chewing the inside of her lip. She had no idea how he would react. Finally she found the courage, "Viktor, husband… I think… I think I'm carrying our first child."
Having now admitted it out loud to her husband she realised another human was growing inside her belly and she began wondering who it would look like. Beside her Viktor was quiet and she cautiously asked, "Viktor?"
She made him stop and stepped in front of him to look up into his face to try and discern his reaction. She saw a tear run down his cheek from behind his velvet mask. She reached up, "oh Viktor?"
  "I will never see him or her smile." He murmured.
  "But you are happy aren't you?"

He nodded, "I am, I am." He smiled, "I am glad." He searched for her lips with his fingers and kept them there as he bent to kiss her lips. Perhaps he should try and make more of an effort to be a good husband to Katerina.

CHAPTER 20

1758

It wasn't an easy pregnancy for Katerina. She spent most of it feeling tired, queasy and bloated. The one positive was that Viktor left her alone and didn't call her to his bedroom. The birthing pains started in the afternoon but the contractions didn't fully start till late in the night when her maid went to report to the Countess as ordered, leaving Katerina with the midwife.

Daria went to the birthing mother. Alla, pulling a robe around her body, appeared at her door having heard the running servants, "what is going on father?"
Tverdislav had been woken as well, "Katerina is giving birth."
"Viktor's not here." She pointed out.
"Where is he?"
"Out at Orianenbaum. He's there a lot these days." Tverdislav frowned. What was his son getting involved in? He had heard about the scraps the Prussian soldiers found themselves in when out in the city. He really didn't want Viktor involved with them but wasn't going to stop his son as it made him happy. But now was not the time to be worrying about that. He said, "we need to get him sent for."
"Of course."
"You can go back to bed if you want."
"I'm awake now." Alla answered as she sat on the settle in Viktor's day room while a servant brought the fire back to life. "I heard a footman grumbling about going out in the snow to fetch the doctor. Why did it have to happen so late in the night?"

"A child decides when it comes. It is God's will. I should go and find out why the doctor is needed." Tverdislav remarked.

"Let's wait."

He sighed, "there are far too many dominating women in this family. You all get it from your mother." He gave his daughter a tight smile. Both of his surviving daughters had taken after their mother in both looks and strength of personality though now there was only Alla.

She laughed, "you married the wrong person then."

"That I did not do." He said sternly, "do not talk of your mother like that. She brought all four of you into this world strong and healthy. Because of her you are here."

"Sorry father." She bowed her head.

With a kinder tone he added, "you are a good girl really. Now, for the time being we must be patient. It's not mine and I'm nervous." Soon might be the next generation to keep the family going. He had prayed many times that his daughter-in-law would give birth to a boy.

Downstairs the door opened and shut and there were footsteps on the stairs. Father and daughter glanced at each other and hoped it might be Viktor but knew it was too soon for him. The Count stood and crossed the room and watched as the doctor was shown into Katerina's rooms by his wife. A long primal moan came through the open door. Tverdislav asked, "what is happening?"

"You don't need to know for the moment." She frowned at her husband and shut the door.

Within Katerina's room the doctor looked round with its many lit candles and blazing fire. A birthing stool sat ready for the new mother to use when the time came. He shrugged his coat off and rolled up his sleeves to try and cool down. The heat made the metallic smell of blood mixed with sweat overwhelming. He asked, "how does it

go?"
The old woman looked up, her hands and clothes already stained with blood, "not well. I fear that she will not give birth naturally. She is already tired."

"Cutting her open should be the last option."

"I know."

"The child is more important than the mother." Daria decreed.
A wail came from the bed and everyone's attention returned to the young mother. A maid wiped her face and throat with a damp cloth.

Katerina was still struggling in labour when dawn broke behind leaden clouds.

Koplev pulled Viktor, half awake, through the front door, trying not to slip on the icy step. Inside Viktor stretched and yawned, having only just woken up from the sledge journey back from the Peterstradt fortress. Entering his rooms he sensed eyes on him and he asked, "what's going on?"
Alla and his father looked over as his sister said, "Katerina is in labour. We sent a messenger."

"Must have missed each other. Is there anything I need to do?" He asked with only a hint of concern. Childbirth was a woman's domain; every man knew that.

"You sit and wait." His father said, "breakfast is about to be served."

"Excellent, I'm starving." Viktor made his way to his table, oblivious to the looks between father and daughter. Alla asked, "are you not even a little concerned? She is in her room giving birth to your child."

"Is she alone?"

"Of course not."
He shrugged, "a birthing chamber is no place for a man."

"Leave it Alla. He is right. We would just get in the

way." Her father remarked as breakfast was served to them.

The evening arrived and there was still no arrival of the baby. Herbs had been thrown on the fire to try and disguise the stench in the room. Katerina lay on her bed worn out and weakening. The midwife and doctor looked at each other as the old woman said, "we must do it. We must cut her open and hope the child is still alive."

"Prepare her then." The sweating doctor said as he wiped his brow with his handkerchief. He washed his hands in the wash bowl and dried them on the towel held by the maid. He rummaged in his bag and found his knives.

Though her eyes drooped they widened as her night gown was pulled up to expose her belly. Maids held her down as she said though ragged breaths, "just do it. I can't stand it anymore. I don't want it in me anymore."

"This won't take long." The doctor remarked as he received the required nod from the Countess. He drew in a deep breath as he sliced into Katerina's belly.

She screamed and then fainted. The doctor cut deeper to open the womb. He drew out the baby which barely stirred as he handed it to the midwife and then cut its umbilical cord. It lay limp in her hands. She wrapped it in an old blanket and began to rub life into it until there was a wail from its tiny mouth. Everyone released their held breaths. Daria demanded, "what sex is it? Will it live?"

"Madam, it's a boy." The midwife declared, "and only God knows if he will live."

"Fetch the wet nurse." The Countess ordered the maid before leaving the doctor stitching up Katerina.

She crossed to her son's sitting room where he waited with Alla and his father. She burst in with a smile surprising them all. Tverdislav rose to his feet, dropping his cards on the table, "well?"

"It is a boy, congratulations Viktor."

Tverdislav sank back into his chair with relief.
Viktor was speechless, "I… And Katerina?"

"She is tired, let her rest." She lied. It was in God's hands whether she would survive or not and then whether she would be able to bear another child.
He accepted what his mother said and asked, "can I hold my son?"

"Soon."

Shortly the wet nurse came in carrying the baby swaddled up. She curtseyed as Daria came and took the baby from her. The Countess smiled down at the now fed and sleeping baby, the next heir, unmarked and not blind. He looked perfect and even had normal blonde hair unlike her son. She took the baby to her son. She sat beside Viktor and carefully put the baby in its father's arms. Cautiously Viktor ran a finger over the child's face. He felt the face wrinkle up and the mouth open as it began wailing. The Countess hastily took the baby back and handed it to the wet nurse who disappeared out of the room.

Those few moments had frightened Viktor. How could he look after his son when he couldn't see him? How would his son react to him when he was older? Would he be seen as an embarrassment like his mother did? He was brought out of his thoughts by his mother, "you must decide on his name and we must get him baptised. I will sort out godparents for him."
No one objected to the Countess taking command of the situation. She went on, "now it has been a long day for everyone and I think we should go to bed."
She gazed at her son and wasn't sure about his reactions to it all. He hadn't demanded to see Katerina. She had hoped for him to be more concerned for his wife than he was but there again maybe it was a good thing. If Katerina died then they could quickly find him another wife. One child was not enough.

Her husband, once alone with her, demanded to know what was going on with Katerina. She reluctantly revealed the truth, "she had to be cut open."

"And will she live?"

"I don't know."

"Do you care?" He challenged her.

She couldn't look her husband in the eye. She had what the family needed now and if Katerina died she would find her son another wife if they needed to. They had the heir they needed. If no suitable wife could be found then Viktor could be hidden away in his rooms again and Society could once again forget about him. He didn't need to visit the Grand Duke's Germans. He didn't need to be anywhere but his rooms, safe, where she could watch over him again.

"And Viktor?" He enquired, "when are you going to tell him?"

"When Katerina either lives or dies. I don't want him to have a fit." She answered, convinced she was doing the right thing for her son.

"He needs to be able to prepare himself. He needs to know that she might die." He suggested, remembering his son's reaction at Tamara's death and not being told.

"I am his mother and know best." She said firmly.

He sighed and submitted to his wife. This was not the time and place for a fight. He would save his energy and strength for when he really needed it.

Viktor sensed there was something amiss as he stood beside the font with his sister close by. He knew Katerina wasn't with them in the church. He had asked to see her but hadn't been allowed. He could have made Koplev take him to his wife but found himself not that bothered. He was more fascinated by his son.

His grip tightened on Alla as he heard his son wailing after having been submerged in the cold water of

the font. She murmured, "it's all right. Aleksei is all right."
The wail paused as Aleksei was immersed again as the
priest said, "the servant of God, Aleksei Viktorovich, is
baptised in the name of the Son, amen."
The child was submerged for the third time, "of the Holy
Spirit, amen."
Alla softly said, "I'll be back in a moment."
Viktor stiffly nodded his head as he let go of his sister so
she could circle the font three times with Aleksei's
godfather, one of Katerina's brothers who was looking
ashen and worried for his sister.

 The baptism in front of family and a few close
friends was soon over and they all returned to the
Medevdev home for a quiet dinner. Many glanced upstairs
as they entered, aware that the mother was upstairs fighting
for her life. Liv Antonovich disappeared upstairs to see his
daughter.

 They all looked up from their dinners and tried to
keep their conversations going as the house steward bent to
the Countess and a maid stood by the door looking worried,
clutching her apron in fidgety hands. They were aware of
the empty seat that was Count Liv Antonovich. The
Countess rose and left the room. Viktor heard her leave and
asked Alla, "what is going on?"
Alla glanced at their father. No one had any real idea how
Viktor was going to react since it had been such a strained
marriage. He gave her a nod. To her brother she said, "let's
get you to your rooms."
He frowned behind his mask, "why?"

 "Please Viktor, don't make a fuss."

 "You are all keeping something from me." He
challenged, "why do you do this to me?!" He fought Alla's
hold of him.

 "Viktor!" His father exclaimed, silencing his son. Once
Alla had led Viktor from the room he gave the families a

tense smile, "please excuse my son, it has been a stressful as well as joyous time. We are all praying for Katerina's survival."
There were murmurs amongst the guests at the news that many were not aware of.

Upstairs Viktor demanded, "get your hands off me." He threw Alla's hold off him, "what are you not telling me? Tell me otherwise I'll never trust you again." His hands were fists and if he could feel for a piece of furniture he would have turned it over.

"Will you calm down before you have a fit if I tell you?" Alla cautiously asked while also afraid of her brother.

"I will try." He gulped as he fought his outrage, "please. There is something amiss with Katerina isn't there?"
She nodded, "yes. They had to cut her open to get Aleksei out."

"Oh." He reached out for a piece of furniture to hold him up. Alla grabbed him as he sank to the floor.

"It is looking like she won't survive." She softly said as she crouched beside him.

"Can you take me to her?"

"Of course."

Daria frowned at her daughter as Alla brought Viktor into Katerina's bedroom. She hissed, "what is he doing here?"

"He needs to know the truth." Alla declared, confronting her mother.
The Countess' eyes narrowed at her daughter but allowed her to take Viktor to the bedside.

Cautiously he reached out for his wife's hand as his nose wrinkled up at the smell of death and sickness in the room, "Katerina?"
She stirred, "Viktor?"

"I'm here. I'm sorry I haven't been a very good husband." He felt his eyes watering. He hadn't been a good husband.

He had used her and ignored her and only now was he
realising what he was about to lose. Soon he would be on
his own again and selfishly he didn't want her to die and
leave him on his own especially as he no longer had
Nastasia either. He had heard she had a new man in her
bed. She had moved on like he had been forced to.

"Thank you for giving me the chance, no matter how
short a time it has been, to be a mother." She replied
through breaths full of pain. She knew she wasn't going to
last much longer. She had held out long enough to hear that
her son had been baptised. Now she knew if he died he
would safely end up in the loving presence of God. She
smiled and squeezed Viktor's hand weakly. He raised the
clammy hand to his lips and kissed the back of it, "forgive
me."

"I forgive you."

"Come on Viktor, you shouldn't be here." His mother
said, "being here will not do you any good."

"I'm staying." He snarled and she retreated, taken by
surprise.

It was another hour before Katerina accepted her
death. Her maid wailed. Tears silently rolled down Alla's
face as she realised she had just lost a friend. Everyone
warily looked to Viktor to see how he was reacting.

He had withdrawn his hand from his wife's. They
couldn't see any tears. Stiffly he said, "I'm going to my
rooms. Sir, I am sorry that you have lost your daughter."

"Thank you Viktor." Count Liv Antonovich responded
stiffly as he fought tears himself. He had just lost his
daughter but a good thing had come out of it with another
grandson for his family.

Daria watched her son leave the room while trying to work
out how he was feeling. She followed him, she wanted to
be ready for anything.

He felt no particular emotion. He hadn't loved her

enough to feel the need to weep or rage over the injustice of it. He was rapidly submitting himself to being alone again.

He shrugged his mother off as she tried to guide him to his chair. She said, "you shouldn't be alone."

"I will be fine." He replied sternly.

"But you've just lost your wife. You might have a fit."

"I didn't love her and feel nothing. Just leave me alone." He snapped and didn't yield to his mother pressing him into his chair.

"Viktor!" She said with warning, "do not say such things. Her spirit may hear you."

"Let it. She probably knew how I felt." He shouted.

"You are having a fit." She said with concern, hurt by his words. She touched his shoulder but he rejected her.

"I'm not. I don't want your pity. I don't need you. I am not a helpless child. I can look after myself."

"No you can't." She found herself shouting back. "You are blind. You'll always need someone."

"And maybe I did have someone…" He fell silent as he felt tears forming.

"Yes you did." She said softly thinking he was referring to Katerina, "and you still have me and Alla."
This time he let her sit him down.

CHAPTER 21

He gave his wife the courtesy of mourning her for the forty days until the uneaten bread and glass of vodka showed that her spirit had ascended to God's Presence. He played with his empty glass as he remarked to the room on the forty-first day after Katerina's death, "I'm sick of this place. The silence is drowning me Koplev. You are a man of the city aren't you?"

"Sir?" Koplev wasn't sure where the conversation was going and wondered whether he should have watered the wine more than he had.

"I'm going to go out and you, man, are taking me."

"Where to?" Koplev asked cautiously.

"Somewhere where the girls are clean. Get the carriage ready and then we are going out."

Koplev bowed, "yes sir."

The servant left the room not sure what to make of the man he served any more. In the last year he had become surer of himself and discovered the joys of being a man and then a husband. Clearly, having been with Nastasia Balakina had given him a sexual appetite that Katerina had not been able to fulfil. Hopefully he would also discover the joys of being a father when the boy was old enough to be engaging.

He wondered if his master would remarry. He had a suspicion that the Countess wanted to keep her son to herself. She had the next heir she needed. Perhaps like the Empress she would claim the baby as her own and leave Viktor to his own devices but this time the man knew of the world outside of his rooms. Meeting up with the Holstein regiment and the Russian officers that hung out with them was probably better than prostitutes and Nastasia in turn would be even better, but it seemed his master no longer thought of her and he thought it a shame.

He told the driver where to go and it stopped outside a house on a quiet side street. The front door opened as Koplev helped Viktor from the carriage. The madam, an older woman clinging to her looks smiled at her potential customers, "welcome, welcome, come in from the cold and snow."
As they entered her hallway there were giggles from the drawing room where a few men were already being entertained by the ten girls that were owned by the madam. She asked, "what can I do for you fine gentlemen?" Discretion kept her from revealing she knew who stood before her.

"Two girls and a bed." Viktor stated with an excited lick of his lips, "my servant can have one as well and then you are to return home Koplev and hide my absence."

"Certainly." The woman smiled. She called into the drawing room, "Polina, Regina, Tatyana. Come and attend to your duties."
Three young women broke away from the party and appeared dressed in low cut linen bodices and flounced skirts. An hour before they had been fully dressed until the first group of customers had arrived to be titillated.

With dulled senses from too much wine earlier in the evening Viktor was led upstairs by two of the girls who had taken whispered instructions from the madam. The other led Koplev down the hallway to a smaller plainer bedroom for servants who were being treated by their masters.

The two blonde haired girls, hair trailing down their backs, led Viktor to a warm room holding a hand each. It's red and gold walls matched the bedding on the pine bedstead. They took off all his clothes before pushing him on to the bed naked with a giggle. They tried to take off his mask but he stopped them, "not that."

They pouted but obeyed.

He reached out and found one of the girl's heads and drew it towards his face while the other straddled him and ran her hands over his chest. The touch of their fingers and lips on his bare skin made him moan with growing anticipation. He grabbed at the girl's hips as she lowered herself on to his erection.

He lost himself in the attentions of the two girls, drowned himself in kisses, their touches, their breasts. He didn't want to think about the real world, just the fantasy that the two girls could give him. At some point he must have cried as his eyes felt dry behind his mask and they had been kissed away by one of them as the other one stroked his face and hummed a lullaby.

He didn't remember falling asleep, with them curled up either side of him, but he must have, mentally and physically exhausted. He had let them wipe away his thoughts of Katerina, of death, of his mother, even of the Holsteins. For a few hours he had forgot all about them, consumed with desire for more primeval needs.

Downstairs Koplev spent an hour with his treat before returning home. The house steward was waiting for him when he slipped in via the servant's entrance, "they want you upstairs. Be careful, she's off on one. One day she'll accept he's a man."

"Thanks for the warning." He was glad that the house steward was on his side, "Where are they?"

"In his study."

Soon he was stood before the Count and Countess. The Count was at his desk while she was by the fire. Tverdislav didn't look at all interested in the servant before him. The Countess glared at him, "let me remind you that though you are Viktor's servant you still answer to myself and my husband."

"Yes madam."

"Then where is he?" She demanded.

"I was doing as he ordered." Koplev replied stiffly.

"I know you left with him." She said accusingly, "Where is he?"

"Daria," the Count decided to enter the conversation, "I think you should stop interrogating him before you embarrass all of us. I think I know where he is and you don't really need to know."
She turned on her husband and glared at him, "don't interrupt Tverdislav Vadimovich. You men all spend your lives plotting together."

"Koplev go." The Count calmly said as he stood to stretch his legs. He crossed to the window and looked out on the dark street and watched a carriage go by with its lamps lit, "and don't forget where my son is or you'll receive my wrath which is worse than my wife's."

"Yes sir." Koplev bowed and then left, shaking slightly at his close call. He took a deep breath once the door was shut.

With the servant gone Daria turned accusingly on her husband, "you know where he is? Why didn't you stop him?! A demon must have possessed him."

"No demon has possessed him Daria." Tverdislav remarked calmly.

"I didn't bring him up to visit whore houses."

Tverdislav looked at her outraged expression, calm in comparison to her. He picked up his tea from his desk, "please let me point out a few things to you. Our son is no longer a child and hasn't been for a long time. He has now been married and has his own child. He has felt freedom and an independence in the last year you never let him have before. He has discovered what it's like to be a man so let him enjoy it."

"Hmpfh." She crossed her arms and appeared to be sulking.

"Daria, stop this nonsense. We need to give him that freedom though he will always need us."

"He should be mourning Katerina's death."

"He will be in his own way."

"We should get him married again as soon as possible." She said with determination, "one heir is not enough."

"No!" Tverdislav responded fiercely, "he will come to us when he is ready."

"We can't just have Aleksei. There is so much that yet might happen." She protested, thinking of what had happened to Viktor and even his brother, lost to the river.

"I know." He sighed heavily as he realised he wasn't getting through to his wife.

"Maybe he will come back to us when we go to the estate." She said to reassure herself.

"Go to bed Daria. There is nothing you can do for the moment."

"He's not going to get away with this." Daria announced as she accepted his hand to rise her to her feet.

"Well, I have warned you dear. He has some of your temper." He remarked as he led her through the door his manservant had opened. She scowled at him and swept pass him leaving him standing on his own.

With the morning Viktor had to think for a moment before he remembered where he was. He smiled as he recalled what had happened overnight. It had been a good night. He had found he had missed having a responsive woman under and above him. He had enjoyed hearing the women responding to his touch with fingers, lips and tongue. Katerina, God keep her well, had been like a plank compared to the two whores withering on and under him.

170

He moved and felt one warm body pressed against him and an arm over his legs. He lifted his mask to rub sleep from his eye. The one at his side stirred, "do you wish for more sir?"

"No. Go and find out if my servant is here and the other can help me dress."

"Yes sir." The one curled round his feet slipped off the bed and pulled on her dress before going downstairs.

Reaching home he willingly sank into his chair with a hand to his head. He had drunk too much vodka and wine the night before. He heard the door open and recognised his mother's footsteps. He moaned as his real life returned to his attention. He really didn't want to have to deal with his mother at that moment in time. He was glad he couldn't see her expression as she remarked angrily, "serves you right. I hope you are now feeling guilty about what you were doing last night."

"Go away." He moaned.

"I'm going nowhere." She stood before her son with her arms crossed, "have you no respect for your wife?"

"She's dead. You let her get cut open for the baby. You cared as much for her as I did and that's not much."

"How dare you?! She was like a daughter to me."

"What about your actual daughter by blood, Alla?"

"She has everything she needs. Don't change the subject. I am here to talk about you and your behaviour. You visit those Germans and do what? I don't know and last night… whores?!"

"I need some pleasure in this miserable life. I am no child. I am a man." He pointed out angrily. He stood to his true height, and she realised he was as tall as his father.

"Your reputation will be affected now that you came home in daylight. How will I find you another wife?" She said accusingly.

"It doesn't matter." He retorted fiercely.

"It does Viktor." She tried pleading.

"Why don't you just tell me how to do everything since you seem to think I can't do anything?!" He challenged, his hands were fists.

"It's only because I love you." She murmured. Tverdislav had been right; Viktor had her temper and she couldn't pretend it wasn't a fit this time. She felt defeated as she watched her son carefully walk away from her. He had never done that before.

CHAPTER 22

1762

On a late spring day he was out walking the Summer Garden on Alla's arm with Alla's new beau at their side, and with a cane in his free hand. He and Dimitri Peterovich were talking which made Alla happy. She liked the fact they got along. The friendship with her future husband was good for him as within the court sides were being created between the new Tsar and the Grand Duchess Catherine.

Everyone was holding their breath to see which way the wind turned. She knew, from conversations with her brother, that their family was keeping quiet. They might be nobility but were so low down their opinion was not of anyone's interest. All the family needed was to ensure that whoever won bought their building supplies and paid their bills. She liked the fact they talked a lot now, rather than her reading to him.

The nursemaid walked discreetly behind while ahead of them ran Aleksei with Peter, his milk brother.

Alla had managed to persuade Viktor out of his rooms, where he had retreated to with no real desire to leave and had brought Aleksei with them so father and son had time together though the boy had other ideas as he paused to stare up at a statue of Venus and Cupid with Peter. She smiled at the boy who she thought took after Katerina in temperament but after his father in looks. Thankfully his blonde hair hadn't paled to the same tone as Viktor's and it even had a few brown streaks in it. His grey eyes sparkled with the mischievousness of a little boy who was spoilt by his grandparents and saw more of them then his own father.

She frowned as she saw the two children pause before a lady sat on a stone bench. She and Viktor were too far back to identify the lady who sat wrapped in a fur-lined cloak over a green dress. She released a breath of relief as Aleksei and Peter turned towards them, a posy of stolen flowers from the garden in Aleksei's small hand. The two boys ran up to Viktor and Alla. Aleksei grabbed at his father's coat, "papa, papa?"

"What is it Aleksei?" Viktor asked as he and Alla stopped walking.

The child pointed towards the lady on the bench who was now looking their way, "is that mama?"
He had yet to accept that his father couldn't see. He couldn't understand that he couldn't considering everyone else could. He didn't even know what was behind the mask as he never saw his father without it.
Alla frowned with concern, "your mother is dead. What has your nurse been telling you?"

"But she knows you when I said who you were." The boy explained with confusion.

"Did she say who she was?"
Aleksei frowned, "no. But..." He wasn't going to give up. His father should speak to his new acquaintance as she seemed nice. He grabbed hold of his father's hand and pulled it, "come papa, I want you to meet her."

"I don't think we should." Viktor weakly protested but allowed his son to lead him along the path if only to apologise to the ambushed woman.

On the stone bench, the woman held her breath nervously as she watched Viktor Tverdislavich being dragged towards her by his son who had shyly introduced himself and Peter to her. She had been surprised when Aleksei had approached her and asked her why she sat on her own looking sad. She found herself speaking the truth to the wide eyed little boy, "my mother died."

"Oh?"

"His mother is dead as well." Peter declared.

"I'm sorry to hear that." She said with a sad smile, "where is your father?"

"Over there." Peter pointed.

She looked and was surprised at who was further up the path. She knew who it was but asked, her voice shaking a little, "who is your father?"

"Viktor Tverdislavich." Aleksei said with pride that he had finally memorised his father's name.

"I know him." She softly smiled as memories came back of their two months together.

"Shall I get him?" Aleksei asked with a smile of his own.

"No, but thank you."

He didn't listen as he and Peter ran off towards Viktor. She found herself chewing her bottom lip. She wasn't sure she wanted to see Viktor again and bring back memories it had taken a long time to forget.

She got to her feet and brushed tears from her face and straightened her skirts though he wouldn't be judging her appearance. She tucked brown hair behind her ear as she gave Alla a nod as the other gasped in recognition of Nastasia. With a tense smile Nastasia said, "I hope you are well Viktor Tverdislavich. I am sorry about the loss of Katerina. You have a good little boy in your son."

"Nastasia?" Viktor asked cautiously. He never thought he would hear that voice again. He drew his son close to him as he stiffly said, "I hope you are not about to bewitch my son like you did me."

"Not at all. He introduced himself to me." She smiled softly at Aleksei who blushed.

"Are you well?" Viktor politely asked.

"I am." She carefully said.

They fell into silence.

Alla touched her brother's arm, "Dimitri and I will continue on."

"Umm, yes." He continued to keep his face and body facing in the direction of Nastasia. He wondered whether either of them had changed much since those sexually charge months. Hesitantly he asked, "what have you been up to?"

"Here is not really the place." Nastasia said once she'd allowed Alla and Dimitri to continue on their way.
The boys' nurse drew the boys away so Viktor and Nastasia could talk in private.

"Then come to mine."

"I hear you are a regular at the Peterstradt fortress?" She answered, trying to deflect Viktor away from her life.

"Not anymore. Things are happening as I'm sure you are aware of. We cannot be seen to be choosing a side."

"True."
He asked, "and you? Are you married?"

"Umm… No."

"Oh…" Just for a moment there was hope, a hope he had forgotten could exist. Could they have a second chance? He repeated his invite, "please come and visit."

"Are you sure? You know your mother does not like me."

"I am my own man and I say you can visit." He answered firmly.

"Very well. Thank you for the invite. I will come the old way."
He smiled and she wondered what he was thinking.

"I will look forward to it, until then..." He held out a hand.

Shyly she took it and he raised her hand to his lips. She blushed and felt a spark flash through her nerves. She saw him look up. Had he felt it as well? Did they dare start again? Did she really want to open old wounds?

It took a few days for her to find the courage to see Viktor. A part of her didn't want to go near him for fear of rejection but as she currently had nothing to lose… She had her own home thanks to her mother. She was still young and beautiful so could still find a husband of her own choosing. She hadn't sat around waiting for Viktor. She'd had a couple of lovers over the last three years and like her mother had accumulated jewels she could sell or pawn if necessary.

Finally, she felt strong enough to attempt to see Viktor. She knew she needed the strength to be able to leave if they couldn't rekindle their friendship.

She approached the servants' entrance where they appeared to be expecting her. Koplev was sent for. He looked surprised to see her. He remarked, "so the rumour is true."

"Koplev," she smiled, "it's good to see you too."

"What can I do for you?"

"Viktor Tverdislavich invited me over. Is the Countess home?"

"No she isn't and these days tends to leave him be. He is with someone currently."

"Oh?" She was disappointed.

"I'll think you'll scare her away." He confined with a chuckle. He knew who he preferred.
She smiled at the compliment, "take me upstairs then."

Entering the room she stopped and eyed the scrap of a girl with brown hair tumbling over her shoulders and a nose, in Nastasia's opinion, that was too big for her face. She didn't seem to have much of a body either, looking on the thin side. So this was his latest. She knew he had had a few lovers, not many as he preferred the brothel, because of the circles she moved in, and she knew he had never kept them for long.

The young woman dressed in a bodice and chemise

stared nervously back from over Viktor's shoulder as she sat straddling his lap. Viktor turned his head at the sound of the door. His young lover spoke first, "who are you?"

"So you are his latest play thing?" Her chin lifted and she daringly said, "and you are the one he put aside?"

Before there were any more barbed comments Viktor interrupted, "Nastasia? I thought you would never come."

"I apologise for the delay. I have been busy." Nastasia lied as she stepped further into the room.

"Faina, you may leave. I will send you a message when I wish to see you again." Viktor calmly informed the girl as he stood to greet Nastasia. Faina slipped off his lap and landed on the floor.

The girl glared at Nastasia for interrupting her afternoon with Viktor as she quickly got dressed and then left. She knew she wasn't going to get paid.

With her gone Nastasia, trying to keep her dignity, crossed to where Viktor stood. She took off his mask as she said with a smile, "there, that's better." On tiptoes she leant up and kissed the scars as he found her hands.

Softly he said, "I never thought I would hear your voice ever again."

"Have any of them satisfied you?"

"You could have come to me once Katerina died." He said, sounding hurt.

"I had moved on as I had to do." She commented as she freed herself from his hands.

"None of them have been able to fill the emptiness in my bed." He admitted, "but..."

"But?"

He held out a hand. She hesitated as she realised what he hinted at. She looked at his tall form and then into his face which looked like he was fighting the same emotions that she was feeling. She decided to risk her emotional and mental well being and placed her hand in his so that he could lead her to the bedroom.

They moved slowly at first. She guided his hands to knots that held her bodice tight. She shrugged out of it and then undid her skirt and underskirt which pooled around her feet. Viktor removed his waistcoat before sinking on to the bed. He reached out and found her arm and pulled her towards him. A giggle escaped as they tumbled on to the bed together and ended up tangled in the unmade bed.

His lips kissed hers and brushed over her throat and down to the ribbon that held the top of her chemise closed, she felt her heart aching for him. Tears ran down her face as she wanted him to be hers for the rest of their lives. She never wanted another man to touch her again. She could survive without marriage as long as she remained only his like her mother had been with her father.

She felt his own need and desire through the urgency in the movement of his fingers and lips. She gasped as he teased her nipples erect with his tongue through the fine linen. His hands swept up under her chemise, pushing it up. She sat up and pulled it off. He gave her seconds to do it before kissing her back down on to the bed.

He wanted to explore every inch of her body again, rediscover it, find new spots that would send shivers of pleasure down her spine.

She was responsive to his touch, emitting little sighs and whimpers. She wanted to pull his head up to hers and kiss him but then she felt his cool breath on her sex. She arched her back and moaned, "I didn't think I would feel like this again."

"Ssh." He murmured softly between her thighs.

He reached up and pressed her down with a hand as he sucked and licked at her little sensitive nub. Now was not the time to be talking about feelings. He wanted her body and soul and for her never to leave again and he would show it through her body first. He sat back on his heels and his fingers found her opening and guided his erection into its hot wet interior.

She rose up so she was sat on his knees and they clung to each other as they moved slowly together, their breaths mingling as they kissed. She didn't know what he was thinking but at this moment she never wanted to leave. She wanted her body to mould itself to him so they were always a perfect fit, and he would have no reason to go looking for another to fulfil his needs.

They broke apart after they had come, panting. She pulled a blanket from the tangled bedding over their half naked bodies and lay against him, her head resting on his shoulder. He kissed the top of her head as she murmured, "I only want to be with you."

"Ssh."

"I hate my life. They just use me but..."

"I have used you just as badly." He softly pointed out.

"What about now?" She cautiously asked.

"I don't want to now, but we do need to decide what we are doing. We both have others to consider." He rolled on to his side and a finger explored her face. She teasingly snapped at his finger when it found her lips.

"Do you think we are meant to be together?" She suggested.

He kissed her as an answer and drew her further under the blanket.

They would willingly have stayed in bed all afternoon but as soon as Viktor was softly snoring she slipped out of his bed. She dressed herself and glanced down at Viktor before leaving the room, the corners of his mouth twitched as he smiled in his sleep.

Viktor willingly abandoned his new mistress and Nastasia became an almost daily visitor. It felt right to be with him and as well as rekindling the sex they discovered a friendship that had been hidden and lost the last time they had been together. They felt comfortable. It felt right. They talked and laughed and Aleksei was allowed to join them. He sat on his father's lap and listened intently as Nastasia read to him and his father.

And they didn't stay inside either. Almost as if she had brought him back to life, he let her draw him outside. They walked the palace gardens with and without Aleksei. There were whispers amongst the gossiping nobility who had almost forgotten who Viktor was and then talked about the woman on his arm.

Two months into their re-acquaintance she sat on the floor with Aleksei playing knucklebones. She looked up at Viktor and smiled to herself. She hadn't felt as happy as this for a long time. She felt like she, Viktor and Aleksei were a family and then she thought of the one growing inside her. She wondered whether she should let him know yet.

In his chair Viktor felt her lean against his leg and he remarked, "we can always send him back to his rooms."

"He's all right." She reached up and took hold of his hand and gave it a squeeze.

He smiled as he thought about the changes in her. There was a calmness and dignity about her from having accepted her fate. As she spent time with Aleksei he felt there was a maternal air about her and she treated him like a man. Then there was the sex. Katerina had only ever obliged in bed whereas when he and Nastasia were together they wanted to satisfy each other. He wondered whether he had changed. An idea came to him, "Nastasia?"

"Hmm?" She answered as she threw the sheep knuckles

up and missed them all making Aleksei giggle.

"I would like to think that you would agree that we have probably both changed for the better… So… would you consider marrying me and becoming Aleksei's mother?" She said after a moment's silence, "I have something to tell you then." She turned to look at him, resting her hands on his knees so she could watch his reaction, "I think I carry your child."

That stunned him. He hadn't expected that, "are you sure it is mine?"

"Yes." She said with certainty.

"Well… will you bear it in wedlock then?" He smiled as he reached for one of her hands on his knees.

"I will." She beamed as she got to her feet and kissed him. She was pleased he had asked her and he was pleased that she had agreed to marry him. He felt sure she would be lover, wife and mother in equal and eager abundance.

At their feet Aleksei looked up at the two adults with wide eyes. One minute she had been playing with him and now she was kissing his father. He tugged at Nastasia's skirt, "hey! Play with me."

"Aleksei." Viktor said with a smile.

"Yes papa?"

"How would you like Nastasia to be your mother and live with us?"

"Will she be able to play with me?" She crouched down and with a smile said, "whenever you want." She looked back at Viktor and asked with concern, "what about your parents?"

"I'll speak to them later. Masha, please take Aleksei back to his rooms." He wanted time alone with Nastasia now. Aleksei's nurse approached, "yes sir, come Aleksei." Aleksei pouted but let himself be herded from the room. Then he remembered his companion and skipped off to play soldiers with him.

CHAPTER 23

His parents and Alla noticed a change in Viktor as Koplev led him to the dining table. He stood taller and had a smile dancing on his lips. No one said anything at first, hoping that he would reveal his thoughts. Finally he couldn't contain it any longer, "mother, father, I have decided to remarry."

The Countess' eyes widened in surprise. She glanced at her husband to see if he was aware of anything as their son tended to confide in him more. Tverdislav shook his head at his wife as he asked, "have you found someone or would you like us to find someone?"

"There is someone."

"Oh?"

Daria worked out who it was then and objected, "no!" She had been made aware of her reappearance in her son's life and had hoped it was just another phase. She had restrained herself from challenging her son on the matter but not anymore.

All the servants looked over. They knew the Countess had a temper but this was the first time in a while it had shown itself at the dining table. The Countess went on, "no way am I allowing you to marry that Balakina slut, not even if I died tomorrow."

"I am and I will and she's no slut." Viktor's voice rose to match his mother's.

The servants prepared to save the china and table centrepieces as they knew Viktor might choose to knock it off the table in his rage.

Trying to defuse the situation and with one eye on the nervous servants. Tverdislav said calmly, "Daria, let us hear him out. Viktor, please, go on."

Viktor inhaled and exhaled a deep breath to calm

himself, "I married the woman of your choice the first time and now I have found my choice. You cannot stop me as I have already asked her."

"But..." Daria started, thinking that she could stop it but shut her mouth as her husband glared up the table at her.

"We are happy together and she carries my child. Aleksei needs a mother and he sees Nastasia as it and she wants to be his mother. Before you say anything mother, she is not after anything more than the love and security I want to give her. She has changed, you should talk to her."

"Pah. How can you trust her? What if she goes back to her old ways? How would we know any child she bore was yours?" The Countess argued.

"She never wanted that life. I know I can trust her." He said firmly while hiding his fists, from his growing anger towards his stubborn mother, under the table.

"I'm not agreeing to her bastard child becoming legitimate or her having the family name." The Countess declared.

"Daria!" The Count interrupted again in exasperation, "if that is what he wants then I'm not going to stop it. God has already blessed the reunion. I want our son to be happy, don't you?"

"Of course I do, but not with some whore." She replied stiffly.

Alla whispered into the tense silence, "she has changed, and I want Viktor to be happy and I am glad he has found someone."

"Thank you Alla." Viktor smiled in her direction.

"I think you are going to have to relent my dear." Tverdislav remarked with a smirk.

"Hmpfh." Daria glared at her plate.

Dinner continued in silence to the servants' relief. Daria quietly seethed. She wasn't going to let Nastasia get away with joining the family. She felt threatened by the strong young woman. Somehow she would get rid of her and the bastard child.

There was none of the splendour of a big wedding when Nastasia and Viktor received the blessing of the rings and then made their way up the aisle for the marriage ceremony. They had agreed there was no point in having an engagement.

There were few guests to witness the marriage of Nastasia and Viktor before God. Tverdislav and Alla were there, keeping a tight hold of Aleksei who wanted to be beside his father and new mother.

Nastasia's father was also discreetly there. He was quietly glad his illegitimate daughter had found her way out of her mother's life before it was too late and she looked so happy as she walked round the altar. He had given the wedding his blessing by acknowledging Nastasia was his daughter. He thought that Nastasia and Viktor looked even better then when it had been Viktor and Katerina. It may have just been the candle lit church but there seemed to be a shimmering aura about them as if God was blessing their reunion. Life had thrown both of them challenges but it looked like He had just made them stronger. He silently prayed that she wouldn't also die in childbirth. He didn't want to lose both of his daughters that way.

Tverdislav's thoughts weren't properly on the ceremony even though once again he held the crown above his son's head. He felt that Viktor had shown himself to be one of those men who could love women indiscriminately for who they were inside rather than what they looked like. And as for Nastasia, she still looked stunning and she even seemed to glow from the pregnancy.

It was a shame that Daria had declined to come. If she had he felt sure she would have found herself changing her mind. She would have sensed the sincerity in the vows made and would have observed the genuine adoration on Nastasia's face. She would also have seen the eager way Aleksei ran to Nastasia as the ceremony came to an end. Nastasia was being a positive influence on both father and son.

It was a sober dinner, no public table, just the wedding guests. No one objected to Viktor being maskless though Count Liv Antonovich did openly stare at seeing the scarring.

The quiet celebrations hopefully deterred the evil spirits from marring the marriage. The one person who could have brought them with her remained in her room leaving Alla playing hostess and hoping her admirer would get the hint. She did spot him talking to her father and sent a silent prayer of hope up. Nastasia tucked her arm through Alla's and said, "maybe?"

Alla glanced at her new sister, "maybe. I hear father has been paid some of the money owed to us."

After the lasts guests left Tverdislav went to his wife's bedroom. She sat in bed and glared at him as he stood at the end of the bed with his candle, "what do you want?"

"Talk to her and get to know her and you might be pleasantly surprised." He remarked sternly. Over dinner he had spoken with her and had enjoyed the discussion they had ended up having.

"This marriage is a charade." She crossed her arms.

"Why are you doing this?" He enquired. He wanted harmony to return to the house. Even his spinster aunt had come to him with concerns.

"Get rid of the Balakina woman and then I'll be happy."

"Are you really that willing to lose a mother for Aleksei, another grandchild and anger Viktor all over again?" How did her overwhelming need to protect their grown son make

186

her so blind to his needs.

"I'll prove you right."

He sighed and decided to leave her to her silly protests. He hoped she would eventually come round once the child was born.

It was a tense summer. Everyone seemed to be falling for Nastasia's charms causing Daria to hate her even more. She felt that Nastasia was taking her family and authority away from her. She was proving herself to be a good stepmother, wife and mistress to the servants.

Daria was desperate to find fault in Nastasia and put her down but Nastasia seemed to be able to cope with her barbed comments. She didn't hear how Nastasia was once behind closed doors, for not even the Countess' own maid mentioned the gossip as they were fond of Viktor's new wife. Like the Countess they were protective of their blind young master even though they sometimes made scathing comments between themselves about the whole family. They were glad to see him happy again. There was a lightness about the house apart from around the Countess and they were enjoying it.

Nastasia knew that the Countess didn't like her however hard she tried to placate her. She kept her despair at the situation from Viktor as much as possible. She didn't want to hurt or worry him but after one outburst too many from Daria she decided she had to tell Viktor.

She waited till they were away from the house. They were returning from a party for the younger children of the nobility held at the palace by new ruler of Russia, the Empress Catherine. Peter and Aleksei clutched presents in their hands. All the boys had received lead soldiers and the girls, papier-mâché dolls. The older children had received a book with improving essays from across Europe led by one written by Peter the Great.

Originally Aleksei had sat opposite his father and stepmother but he had quietly slipped across and now sat on his father's lap under the furs while Peter lay asleep on his mother. Aleksei leant against his father's chest with half closed eyes. Nastasia smiled softly as she leant against Viktor as well and took hold of his hand under the furs while the other rubbed at her swollen belly as the baby kicked, "Viktor…?"

"Mmm?"

"Your mother still doesn't like me." She admitted, "I have tried so hard. Is there anything you can do?"

"I have tried myself." He frowned in answer and then went on thoughtfully, "it's all about pride. You'll have to put yours to one side as she won't."

"She thinks I am like my mother but I'm not. I never wanted to be with those men. The thought of you was always at the back of my mind though I didn't realise it until we found each other again."

"I know you are not your mother. You shouldn't worry about it. This is not the time to be worrying about it all. It will harm the baby." He gave her hand a squeeze, "we are a family and that is what matters more to me. I don't know what I would do without you now."

"Thank you." She smiled and then looked at Aleksei again, "I think he will enjoy having a brother or sister."

"Yes and I will enjoy it as well." He said with hints of other desires behind the words making her giggle and blush. He added, "just remember, you are going to have to make the first supplicating move."

"I will take it into consideration." She murmured since she had already tried several times. At least she knew Viktor would always support her.

CHAPTER 24

1763

 She decided to give it one more try before the birth of her child. If it failed, then her last hope was that the Countess fell in love with her new grandchild. With fear heavy on her chest she entered the Countess' private sitting room. Daria glared at her daughter-in-law, "what do you want?"

"Please, I come in peace."

"You are only here for the status." Daria retorted with bitterness.

"I know you only want to protect your son and so do I. I wish to learn from you, how to be a good wife and mother." She nervously clasped her hands together over her stomach, hoping she came across humble enough for the Countess.

"Just get out of my sight slut."

"I carry your grandchild; do you not care about that?"

"It is not his, so it's therefore not mine." The Countess spat, "have your bastard here if you must but then leave and never darken the doorstep again. You aren't wanted in this house. How long will it take you to accept that?"
Fighting back tears Nastasia left the room with as much dignity as she could muster to show that the Countess' comments had not affected her.

 She barely held the tears in as she entered Viktor's sitting room and saw father and son together. Viktor looked in her direction as Aleksei ran over to her with an exclamation of "mama!"
In a voice that was fighting to become a sob she said, "Aleksei, go to your rooms."
He frowned up at her but allowed his nurse to lead him out.
 Viktor heard the strangled sob and asked with fear,

"Nastasia? What's wrong? Is it the baby? Is it coming?"

"No, it's not the baby." She said with a tightly controlled voice.

"My mother then?" He sighed.

The tears fell then as she sat on the settle. She watched Viktor come to her and she leant into his body, "I have tried so hard. I tried to be humble but it didn't work. Maybe I should just go, that's what she wants me to do."

"No." He exclaimed.

"Why don't we go and make our own home."

He hesitated and then reluctantly said, "I would gladly say yes if I had my sight but I will always need my parents and Alla as much as I need you."

"But Alla will be gone soon. There's nothing keeping you here. I have my own money, I can evict the tenants and free up my property, for us." She couldn't understand why Viktor didn't want to leave. He knew what his mother was like. Why couldn't he see further than the four walls of his rooms? Koplev could come with them.

He felt the cold air as she broke away from him. He knew she was angry and frustrated at him but he couldn't leave the house. His home was familiar, the furniture unmoving. He wasn't going to say it to her but he was scared of being in a new place. Would he be able to learn where the furniture was so he didn't constantly bump into it?

Nastasia was relieved once the birth was over and to be still very much alive.

Alla was there the whole time looking a little terrified at the blood and cries of pain that were involved in it all. She knew her own time would come soon enough as was her duty.

Viktor couldn't be stopped from entering her bedroom as soon as he was allowed in by the midwife, and the Count wasn't far behind. The hour old baby wrapped in swaddling was put in his arms. Its little mouth yawned sleepily and didn't react as Viktor ran his fingers lightly over the wrinkly face of the new sleeping baby. Nastasia looked at father and son through half closed eyes and smiled sleepily.

"Well done Nastasia and thank you." The Count beamed. He was happy to have another grandson just in case, God forbid, Aleksei died. Now he just needed to convince his wife to see the child and maybe then harmony would return to the household. He hoped that as a mother many times over herself it would mean she had enough maturity to be able to love an innocence baby however much she might dislike Nastasia.

Sadly that didn't happen and little Mikhail was known as the 'bastard' by the Countess, even in her son's hearing. Viktor and her shouted over the matter many times, ignoring the advice over pride he had given Nastasia. The atmosphere within the house grew tenser and Mikhail sensed it.

Another sleepless night for everyone and the Countess stormed into Viktor's sitting room where Nastasia and the wetnurse were trying to calm the red faced Mikhail. Viktor was out at court with his father supervising the delivery of building supplies for the new Empress' building schemes. She glared at Nastasia who was dressed in a robe over her night gown, "why won't he stop?!"

Nastasia looked up with shock, "he's only a baby."
"Where is my son?"
"Out…" Nastasia tried to remain calm.
"My son needs to be protected. He needs to be kept safe and you can't do that. He could be anywhere out there." Nastasia had to bite her tongue as she knew where Viktor was and she bet Daria did as well.

"He needs to be kept at home so no one can call him a freak and no one can suggest he should have died. He won't be able to hurt himself if he just stayed at home. And you, you encourage him to go out and…." Daria briefly lost steam.

Nastasia opened her mouth to speak but Daria composed herself and held up her hand to silence her, "I want you to leave here, leave the city, go far away from here with your bastard and never return."

Nastasia's reply burst out of her, "you can't see him for who he is. You are a selfish short-sighted bitch who can't see he is an adult with adult needs. I love him and I am the best person for him, not you. Let him go. If you want him to love you, he does but the more you pull him in the harder he will push back. I can see that; your husband can see that. I'm not going anywhere. He needs me, I need him. I'm not taking Mikhail away from his father, his family."

"I'll pay you if I have too. Is that what you want? Money?"

"I don't want or need it."

"Even better."

"And if I don't go?"

"I will find a way to be rid of you." Daria leant into Nastasia's face with a voice full of menace.

Nastasia took a half step back as she tried to hold her ground. She couldn't let the Countess see she was scared though her heart was beating fast in her chest. She wasn't sure whether Daria would carry out the threat or not. Did she even want to hang around and find out?

There was silence. Mikhail had worn himself out with his wailing. Daria stepped back looking smug, crossing her arms. She raised an eyebrow, "well?"

Nastasia chose not to say anything. She hoped her face wasn't revealing anything she was thinking.

Daria turned and stalked out of the room.

Nastasia collapsed into Viktor's chair with a huge sigh of relief. The wetnurse stared wide eyed at her and cautiously asked, "are you alright?"
Nastasia gripped the arms of the chair tight, fearing that if she tried to stand up her legs would go from under her. She finally spoke, "I don't know."
"What she said was terrible. Why doesn't she like you?"
"Because I'm not the daughter in law she wants."
"But you and the young Master are so good together."
Nastasia wanted to thank the young woman but instead said, "take him back to the nursery and let him sleep." The wetnurse nodded and carefully left.

Nastasia let herself cry now she was on her own. She loved Viktor but it was so hard living in the toxic environment created by his mother. She needed time and space, however much it would break his heart, break hers. She would have to take Mikhail with her. She couldn't let him suffer more than necessary because of her. She couldn't go to her apartment, she would have to find somewhere else to stay, perhaps go on a pilgrimage. There must be a saint that could offer her some guidance.

A few days later, while Viktor was sparring with his father she slipped out via the servant's entrance with the wetnurse and Mikhail. The maid didn't know where they were going just that she had to pack clothes for her and Mikhail. Nastasia dressed herself simply in her plainest dress and her fur lined cloak.

Outside she looked back at the house and murmured, "I'm sorry Viktor, I have to. You'll forgive me eventually."
She had left a letter on his table in the window and hoped someone would find it and read it to him.

My Dearest Love,

Hopefully someone is reading this to you.

It is clear that your mother will never welcome myself and Mikhail into your family. I have gone away for a few days. I need to think about me and our son. We can't live as we are. I need to protect him. I don't know if I am going to come back.

I will always love you and Mikhail will know that he was loved by you as well. I promise to dutifully remain your wife wherever I may find myself.

I ask for forgiveness for this act from yourself, Alla and your father.

Nastasia Medevdev.

Alla and Tverdislav looked at each other in disbelief as she finished reading the note aloud. They turned to Viktor. Tears rolled down his cheek and his hands were clenched into white knuckled fists. Anger radiated off him as he grimly remarked, "this is all mother's fault. She must be shown this note as because of her I may have lost my son and wife forever. We need to find Nastasia, now!" He shouted at the end.

"We don't know where she's gone." Alla cautiously pointed out, fearing her brother might turn his anger on her.

"Damn my blindness otherwise I would go out myself." He turned his frustration on himself.

"I'll send some men out now." The Count said to reassure his son.

At that point Daria walked in having heard that Mikhail and Nastasia had disappeared. Her desire to celebrate her triumphant overpowered her maternal instincts to comfort her son. She entered with a smile, "I told you she was using us."

"No!" Viktor stood and shouted, rage rising in him again, "no. She left because of you. You made living here so difficult for her and Mikhail that she had to take my son away from your venom filled words before you harmed him. The fact you come here now crowing over your success shows you don't really care about anyone but yourself. We will find her and then you will apologise to her."

"I bet she won't return even if you find her. She has got what she wanted." The Countess sneered with her own anger. She looked to her husband for support but he didn't give it. He took a step closer to their son, shocking her.

"You lie mother." Viktor snarled, "she tried so hard to earn enough respect from you so that you would leave her alone but you threw all her goodwill back at her. No wonder she left."

"Viktor, you're having a fit." The Countess said.

"No I'm not." He stamped his foot, "father, I think we should start looking. The sooner she is found, the sooner mother can apologise to Nastasia and start calling my son by his actual name."

They didn't find Nastasia that day. They had no idea where she had gone. The Count promised his son they would continue looking the next day as he and Viktor returned home. For the moment the only person outside the immediate family to know that Nastasia was missing was Count Liv Antonovich. He couldn't understand what it was between the two families that seemed to attract and repel each other in equal measure.

Viktor couldn't sleep out of fear for Nastasia and Mikhail. He didn't know where they were and worried whether they were even alive. The nightmare of his childhood came back to him. The bear clawed him as it always did but then it ran away holding a blanket bundle which he knew was Mikhail. Then he was on his knees, blood oozing through his hands, weeping for his child. Around him was laughter, mocking him, and it sounded like his mother's laugh. He moaned and pleaded in his sleep and then sat upright screaming, tangled in his bedding, until he realised he was in his bed and gulped for breath.

He heard his servant's door open and Koplev cautiously asked, "sir?"

"A drink." Viktor gasped while trying to regain his composure.

"Yes sir." Koplev walked through the bedroom and returned moments later with a glass of watered wine left from the previous day.

"You can go now." Viktor said once the glass was in his hand. He downed it and threw the glass at the fireplace. It felt good to do it, releasing some of his frustration.

He forced himself to eat though he didn't feel like eating. But as the week progressed with no sightings or word from Nastasia he started just picking at the food on his plate. Why live without her? It was like his soul had been ripped in half. It was Nastasia who had made him alive and it was her who had brought him and Aleksei together and then turned them into a family.

Forgetting he had Alla and Aleksei with him eating lunch he swept his plate off the table. It smashed on the floor making his sister and son jump. He demanded, "are they still looking? It's been a week, why haven't they found her?"

"Is mama with God?" Aleksei looked scared and was

about to start crying.

Alla drew her nephew to her and softly said, "no she's not."

"She might be." Viktor muttered miserably.

She looked up at her brother and sternly said, "we are still looking Viktor." Then more softly she added, "it's a large city remember. She could be hiding anywhere or she could have even left."

"No, no, no!" He slammed his fist on the table.

Aleksei started crying.

"You must stay strong for her. We will find her." She said sternly, trying to reassure both of them.

CHAPTER 25

Tverdislav had to reread the letter again. He had found her. She was staying at the Yuriev Monastery in Novgorod. She didn't know he had tracked her down.

He told no one where he was going as he didn't want to disappoint anyone if she wasn't there anymore. He urged the carriage driver to go as fast as he could and change horses if necessary. He didn't travel with any spare clothes.

The Monastery was made up of a large garden and two churches inside a white painted and plastered window filled building that also acted as the wall of the complex. The three onion domes of the Church of St George were silver rather than gold. He was lead through the corridors to the archimandrite, the abbot of the monastery. He was made welcome by the abbot and was directed to the beach on the banks of the Volkhov River.

Tverdislav headed down and spotted Nastasia by the water's edge, letting Mikhail experience the lapping water on his bare feet. He paused and smiled. Once Daria had been like that, when they had been more often on the estate than in the city, together. He almost didn't want to disturb her but he had to. She looked at peace and had a healthy glow about her that he realised she had lost from the strain of her relationship with his wife.

He took a step closer, "Nastasia Livovna?"
She looked up and pulled Mikhail to her chest.
He held his hands up, "I come in peace. My wife isn't here. I just want to talk."
"How did you find me? Is Viktor with you?"
"I haven't told him. We have a lot to discuss I think."
She nodded numbly. She let him come to her. He put a

hand on her arm and looked into her face, "how are you?"

"Better."

"And Mikhail?"

"It was the right thing to do." She said stiffly, "he was troubled by the hostility of our situation. Now, he is a happy baby. He's not crying all his frustrations out."

"Shall we walk?" He bent an arm and she slipped one of hers into it.

"Now, I think in comparison to our spouses we are the calm ones, agree?"

"Yes."

"I can't do anything about my wife but I can help you. Your flat is currently being rented and that is your money, your property. Viktor could claim it if he wanted but he has no gains from it and anyway your father has a contract in place to protect it so only you benefit from it. It is why, since the wedding, he has recognised you as his daughter." She nodded.

"Would you come back if I sorted a place of your own out, for you and Viktor?"

"And Aleksi?"

"And Aleksi."

She didn't need to think about it, "of course I would, but Viktor?"

"I think he will see the light." Tverdislav smiled warmly. She smiled back, "I hope so."

"He is lost without you. He's pining for you."

"I should hope so." Nastasia replied, trying hard not to reveal she missed Viktor as well. He had always been the one for her even when they'd been forced apart by Katerina.

"Then that's settled, come home."

Daria sat at her son's table trying to encourage him to have some soup. He continued to stare out of the window, refusing to engage with his mother.

"Please, you need to eat. You need to stop this foolishness. She is not coming back. You are not going to live if you continue to starve yourself."

"And what's the point. You have Aleksei now, you don't need me."

With the strong belief of a mother who knows what is best for their son she repeated again what she had been saying for the last three weeks, quietly gloating to herself and forgetting her son's emotional welfare, "I knew this would happen. I told you but you wouldn't listen. She only married you so that bastard would have a claim to our wealth. It probably isn't even yours."
Viktor found the strength to order, "enough! You are no mother to me so leave me."

"She doesn't deserve you dying over her." In her opinion Nastasia's disappearance with Mikhail was proof that Viktor had made a bad choice. She had shown herself to be a liability and now Viktor needed to get over it, see if he could get the marriage annulled and find himself a better wife. She would find him one more suitable than the whore.

"Stop this mother." Alla said sternly. Her mother turned, surprised at how quietly her daughter had entered.

"Why? I only want what's best for my children." The Countess glared at her daughter. Why could they not see it? Everything she did was for them.

"I don't think so considering you would have let me live here playing nursemaid to our aunt and Viktor. I am so glad I am soon to be married and away from here. And I'll take Viktor and Aleksi with me as well if I have to." Alla protested.

"Ha! You won't have the money to look after them and I had to ensure there was someone to look after Viktor when I die."

"You are not helping him."

"I am going nowhere. I am where I should be, taking care of my son, your injured brother." Daria emphasised the last words. Alla sighed and rolled her eyes in exasperation.

Returning to the peace of her own room where she was sewing parts of her trousseau she paused at the top of the stairs as she heard the front door open. She looked down to see her father guiding a woman clutching a baby through. Her eyes widened, had her prayers been answered, "Nastasia?"

Nastasia looked up and saw the biggest smile on Alla's face that she had ever seen. It gave her the strength she was going to need when she met the Countess again. She hoped Tverdislav would keep his word.

As Alla ran down the stairs Tverdislav took Mikhail from his daughter-in-law's arms; just in time as his daughter embraced Nastasia. Alla stepped back quickly with a wrinkled nose, "you stink. I think you need a wash and change of clothes before you see Viktor."
Hesitantly Nastasia asked, "how is he?"
"We have been travelling Alla." Tverdislav pointed out.
"Where did you find her?"
Tverdislav looked to Nastasia who shook her head. To his daughter he said, "that doesn't matter now."
Alla took Nastasia's hand and dragged her up the stairs, "he will be better once he sees you but come on, lets get you nice and clean and presentable."
Nastasia glanced down but only saw encouragement on the Count's face and love for his grandson who was stirring after being kept asleep by the rocking carriage. His wetnurse stepped forward, ready to claim him so he could be fed.

Once cleaned, her hair brushed till it shone again and in clean clothes Nastasia went first to the nursery. Aleksei ran at her and hugged her legs as he excitedly cried, "mama."

She placed a hand on his head and ruffled his hair as she smiled, "it's good to see you too."

He let go and she stepped past him towards the cradle but it was empty. She turned to Aleksei's nurse, "where is he?"

"Are you looking for Mikhail?" Daria said as she stepped into the room holding Mikhail in her arms. She glared at Nastasia, "how dare you risk my grandson's life by disappearing like that?"

Nastasia frowned in confusion, "but you call him bastard?"

"No, he's Mikhail, my grandson and you are not allowed anywhere near him. You have shown that you are not fit to be a mother."

At hearing mother and baby had been found she had swept into the nursery to see how Mikhail was. She may consider him a bastard but maternal instincts told her it was her son's bastard and now he was back he wasn't going to be allow out of the house again, "we'll have to pray that he lives after your foolishness." She turned and left with the wet nurse trailing behind as Mikhail began crying again.

She was too shocked by the Countess' words to rage and shout as she wanted to. She was frozen to the spot staring at the door and didn't even feel Aleksei take hold of her hand. She felt thankful that soon she would get all of her family out of the Countess' overbearing and hate filled clutches. She was brought out of her angry thoughts by Aleksei tugging at her hand and saying, "come and see papa and make him better."

He dragged her to his father's rooms, crashing through the door. He called out, "mama is back from her trip."

The hunched figure at the table stirred and a voice sighed, "Aleksei, you shouldn't be here. Go back to your rooms."

"But papa..." Aleksei persevered.

Nastasia said softly to the little boy, "Stay here."

He watched her cross the room and take his father's head in her hands. He watched wide eyed as she kissed his father's scarred forehead.

Viktor blinked and tried to focus on the shape in front of him, "Nastasia? Are you a ghost come to haunt me?"

She chuckled, "no."

The laugh faded as she realised how melancholic he was. This wasn't her Viktor. How quickly he had changed and she had only been gone three weeks, "what have you been doing to yourself?"

"Where were you?" He whispered.

"I..."

"It doesn't matter." He murmured with a sorrowful smile. She knelt down at his feet and held tight to his hands, "please forgive me."

"You know you don't need to ever say that. I will always forgive you." He quietly said, still trying to decide if she was real.

"I'm going to get us all away from here, away from your mother and then I will never leave you again, I promise."

"What are you talking about?" He frowned, "this is our home."

"Rest my love and I'll explain when you are stronger." She said softly.

"Where is Mikhail?"

"He is in the nursery. Now, I need to go but I'll be back." She stood and kissed him on the lips. She brushed a tear from his cheek.

He realised she was real.

EPILOGUE

Two months later she walked through the rooms of a large apartment. In their new bedroom she had put Viktor's gift of Saints Peter and Fervonica in pride of place on the wall. Just like the story they had found their way back to each other. She lifted it from its nail and kissed it and whispered as she replaced it, "thank you."

In the rest of the apartment a maid and Koplev was opening all the shutters and throwing open the windows to let the breeze in. The Count had remained true to his promise.

Aleksei careered past followed by Peter and his nurse who briefly paused to dip a curtsey to Nastasia. She smiled benevolently at the servant as they passed each other. Already her mood was lifting now that they were away from her dominating mother-in-law. She looked in on Mikhail who gurgled in his cradle, watching the rainbow from a crystal dance on the ceiling.

She gave the baby a kiss and to herself she remarked, "soon you might have a brother or sister." From the nursery she returned to the sitting room where a masked Viktor sat in his chair, seemingly oblivious to what was going on around him. It hadn't been that hard to convince him that they needed to leave the family home when she returned. He had clearly had enough of his mother as well.

He looked in her direction with a smile, "I think we will be happy here."

"I do too. Aleksei is enjoying himself already. Your father was very generous. There is plenty of room for all of us." She bent and kissed his cheek as she pulled off his mask.

He reached out for her hand, "I'm glad you are happy. Now

we can be a family without mother interfering. Now," he tugged her round and pulled her on to his lap, "let's make this family bigger."
She giggled but didn't reveal her secret.

<u>**Historical Note:**</u>

The first half of the 18th century in Russia was an interesting period brought about by Peter the Great. He did a grand tour of Europe and brought many of the Western European ideas and ideals back with him. Thus began a century of change for Russia where they bounced back and forth between looking to Europe and looking inwards to their old Russian customs. Even within that there were times they looked to the Germanic states and other times they looked to France. Most notably Western Europe influenced their clothing and architecture but their governing and military were also influenced by Peter the Great's grand tour which carried on through his two daughters and then on to Catherine the Great.

What is a fascinating fact is that Empress Elizabeth was the last true Russian Romanov. Her heir, Peter and his wife, known to the world as Catherine the Great, were, between them, 75% German.

I have tried to keep this book in keeping with the era but there has been a little bit of creative licence based on that culturally turbulent time.

<u>**Author's Note:**</u>

As an independent author I would like to thank you for purchasing this book and I hope you have enjoyed it. Thanks goes to Annie Charmer for being a beta reader and guiding me, with her knowledge, on making this a better book.

With no support from a big publishing house every purchase and review mean something to me so please spread the word and write a review. You can find me on Instagram as @f_garstang_author and let me know personally what you thought. You'll also see what I am working on and what will be coming out.

I am a multi genre author and I also have the below out:

Historical: The Crusade's Secrets
Historical Fantasy: Kukulcan's Messenger
Historical with supernatural element: The Dacha in the Forest
Fantasy Series: The Defenders of the Valley
                     The Lost God
                     The Daughters of Scyth
Romance: Biker Leather and Woolly Sheep.

Thank you

www.ingramcontent.com/pod-product-compliance
Lightning Source LLC
Chambersburg PA
CBHW070351200726
48294CB00003B/854